J. P. Lane

# Historical Sketches of the First Congregational Church

Anatiposi

J. P. Lane

# Historical Sketches of the First Congregational Church

Reprint of the original, first published in 1872.

1st Edition 2023 | ISBN: 978-3-38212-811-1

Anatiposi Verlag is an imprint of Outlook Verlagsgesellschaft mbH.

Verlag (Publisher): Outlook Verlag GmbH, Zeilweg 44, 60439 Frankfurt, Deutschland
Vertretungsberechtigt (Authorized to represent): E. Roepke, Zeilweg 44, 60439 Frankfurt, Deutschland
Druck (Print): Books on Demand GmbH, In de Tarpen 42, 22848 Norderstedt, Deutschland

# HISTORICAL SKETCHES

OF THE

# First Congregational Church,

BRISTOL, R. I.,

1687—1872.

BY J. P. LANE, PASTOR.

PROVIDENCE:
PROVIDENCE PRESS COMPANY, PRINTERS,
1872.

# INDEX.

# HISTORY.

## I.

## THE FOUNDATIONS LAID,—1620–1691.

### PRELIMINARY SURVEY OF THE GROUND.

When the Pilgrim Fathers landed at Plymouth, in 1620, MASSASOIT, at the head of the powerful tribe of *Wampanoags* or *Pokanokets* was the principal Sachem of the territory between Narragansett and Massachusetts Bays, having his chief seat at *Sowams* or *Sowamset*, now Warren, R. I.

He early manifested a friendly spirit toward the English, and, in the spring of 1621, made a treaty of peace with GOVERNOR CARVER, which was maintained without serious difficulty until his death in 1661.

He was succeeded by his eldest son, ALEXANDER. A rumor soon after obtained credence that Alexander was not disposed to follow in the good way of his father, but was plotting with the *Narragansetts* against the English. He was promptly summoned to the court at Plymouth, where he stoutly maintained that the rumor was false. Having pledged fidelity he was suffered to depart in peace, and not long after died.

PHILIP, the youngest son of MASSASOIT, succeeded his brother ALEXANDER, having his chief seat at *Mount Hope*, a beautiful elevation on the east side of the peninsula, now included within the limits of Bristol, R. I. Among his first acts, he renewed the ancient treaty of his father with the Colonists, and five years passed away before any suspicion of treachery was entertained, when there was a vague charge that he was willing to plot with the French or Dutch against the English. This he denounced as a calumny. After nearly four years more, another rumor of treachery awakened solicitude at both Plymouth and Boston. Upon investigation, proofs of bad faith were discovered, but conference with the authorities issued in renewed engagements of fealty. Three years later, SASSAMON, a "praying Indian," informed the Governor of Plymouth, that PHILIP was trying to excite other Sachems to war against the English. On hearing of this, PHILIP protested that it was not so, but the government did not believe him. A few days after, SASSAMON was missing, and it was soon discovered that he was murdered at the instigation of PHILIP. Concealment of his treachery being no longer possible, PHILIP openly engaged in war, and, having enlisted the coöperation of other tribes, lighted the flame in various parts of the country which burned so deeply that it proved to be the most terrific of all those early conflicts with the Indians into which the Colonists were drawn. The first English blood was shed on or about the twenty-fourth of June, 1675, and peace was secured under the well-directed energy of the HON. BENJAMIN CHURCH, in command of the Colonial forces, by the death of PHILIP, who was killed near Mount Hope the twelfth of August, 1676, and by the surprise and capture, a few days later, of ANNAWON, PHILIP's chief warrior. The territory over which Philip had presided came into the possession of Plymouth Colony by right of conquest.

When the war thus brought to a close broke out in 1675, Plymouth had been settled fifty-four years, and the entire population of New England, excluding Indians, was about eighty thousand. In what is now the State of Maine, there were thirteen towns and plantations, and one organized Congregational Church. In New Hampshire, four towns and three churches. Vermont had not been settled. Massachusetts had sixty-four towns and fifty-seven churches. Connecticut had twenty-three towns and twenty-one churches; and Rhode Island had six towns, viz.: Providence, Newport, Portsmouth, Warwick, Westerly and New Shoreham, but no organized Congregational Church. The various tribes of Indians had been greatly reduced in numbers by wars among themselves and with the Colonists and by the inroads of disease, and in all did not exceed eleven thousand, of whom about four thousand were "Praying Indians," who had been won to some comprehension and practice of Christianity.

"Along a line of rugged coast, from the Penobscot to the Hudson, were scattered settlements of Englishmen at unequal distances from each other,—closely grouped together about midway of that line, farther apart at the extremities. Almost all of them were reached by tide water. A very few were planted in detached spots in the interior; the most distant of these being about a hundred miles from the sea, whether measured from the east or from the south. In the three associated Colonies there was great similarity in the ordinary occupations and pursuits. The adults of both sexes worked hard; the children went to school. The greater part of the men got a living by farm labor, providing bread and meat, milk, butter and cheese for their own tables, and raising stock to sell in the West Indies for money with which to buy foreign commodities. But they were not all farmers. A portion were lumberers plying the axe through the winter in the thick pine forests, and, at the return of Spring, floating down their rafts to a sure and profitable market. Another portion were fishermen, familiar with the haunts of the cod, the mackerel and the whale, and with all perils of the sea. In the principal towns, various classes of artisans pursued a lucrative trade. The country furnished some staples for an advantageous foreign commerce; and especially in Boston not a few merchants had grown rich."—*Dr. Palfrey's Hist. N. E.*, III. 132, 134.

## SETTLEMENT OF THE TOWN OF BRISTOL.

The treaties of the Indian Chiefs Massasoit, Alexander and Philip, with the Plymouth Colony, secured to them their rights to the land, unless parted with by honorable purchase, but recognized the jurisdiction of the Colony under the English Crown over the entire territory. In 1669, the Plymouth Court granted one hundred acres within the present limits of Bristol, to Mr. John Gorham, "if it can be purchased of the Indians;" and the remainder to the town of Swanzey, "for the promoting of a way of trade in this Collonie." On the first of July, 1672, Mr. Constant Southworth, Mr. James Brown, and Mr. John Gorham were appointed by the Court "to purchase a certain p'cell of land of the Indians granted by the Court to the said John Gorum lying att Pappasquash Neck."* After the close of Philip's war on the thirteenth of July, 1677, the Court "rattified, established and confirmed the aforesaid one hundred acres of land to John Gorum's heirs and successors forever." This land was north of the town Cemetery, between the Neck road and the Bay, and remained in the Gorham name and family for several generations down to a quite recent date.

In 1680, The Plymouth Colony granted to John Walley, Nathaniel Oliver, Nathaniel Byfield, and

---

* *Pappasquash, Poppasquash, Pappoosquaws, Pappasqua.* This name, so variously spelled, has, according to Dr. Trumbull, two plausible derivations; one, from *papasqu*, meaning "double" or "opposite to," applicable to the southern end of Bristol, divided by the harbor; the other, from *paupocksu*, meaning "partridge," applicable to this place as having been a good hunting ground for partridges. Another derivation is from *Pappoose* and *Squaws*, from the fact that in the early Indian wars the *Pokanokets* sent their children and wives to this Neck as a place of safety. This last derivation seems to be now generally accepted, although it is mere speculation, there being no historical data to establish it. The name was at first used to designate all of the western part of what is now Bristol, including both the beautiful peninsula to which it is now applied and the land north, as far as the Warren river.

Stephen Burton, four merchants of Boston, for £1100, all that portion of territory not previously sold, which is now included in the town of Bristol. The whole of Plymouth Colony was then settled, except this territory, which was the last spot left uncovered in the western march of English population. Mr. Oliver sold his share of this purchase to Nathan Hayman, another merchant of Boston.

These gentlemen obtained from the Colony special privileges, and made liberal provisions for the settlement of the town. Among the former were exemption from all Colony taxes for the term of seven years; the privilege of sending Deputies at once, as other towns, according to the number of freemen; a Commissioner's Court to try and determine all actions and causes under ten pounds, with liberty to appeal to the Court of Plymouth; also, when sixty families were settled, a new County should be organized, and this town should be the County or Shire town. Among the latter were the laying out of broad and regular streets, with building lots of convenient size on them; the donation of lands for the support of the Ministry and Schools; the reservation of a large and beautiful Common in the central part of the town; and the donation of six hundred acres for the Common improvement of the settlers, and designated as "The Commonage." The proprietors retained for themselves, each, one-eighth part of the original purchase, and, with the above donations, put the balance into the market for sale at reasonable prices. The liberal inducements offered soon drew a number of families here, chiefly from Boston, where the proprietors resided, and from Plymouth Colony. The proprietors, themselves, also settled here with their families, and closely identified themselves with all the interests of the town. On the first of September, 1681, the people assembled together and agreed "the name of this town shall be Bristol."*

---

*The following names appear on the Town Records, as being admitted Inhabitants at this date:

John Walley, Nathan Hayman, Nathaniel Byfield, Stephen Burton, Proprietors; and Captain Benjamin Church, Doctor Isaac Waldron, Nathaniel Williams, Nathaniel Reynolds, John Wilkins, William Ingraham, Nathaniel Paine, Christopher Saunders, Timothy Clarke, John Saffin, Solomon Curtis, John Finney, Jabez Gorham, Hugh Woodbury, John Rogers, Jabez Howland, Jonathan Davenport, Richard Smith, Joseph Baxter, William Brown, John Corps, Joseph Ford, John Cary, Edmund Ranger, Benjamin Ingell, George Waldron, Thomas Walker, Thomas Dagget, Thomas Lewis, John Pope, John Martin, David Cary, Increase Robinson, William Hedge, Daniel Landon, Widow Elizabeth Southard, Anthony Fry, John Smith, William Hoar, Robert Dutch, James Burrel, Nathaniel Bosworth, Benjamin Jones, Eliashib Adams, Zechariah Curtis, John Gladding, Joseph Jacob, Robert Taft, Peter Pampelion, Samuel Woodbury, Samuel Gallup, James Burrows, Uzal Wardwell, Benjamin Bosworth, Edward Bosworth, Samuel Penfield, George Morye, Jonathan Finney, Nicholas Mead, Jeremiah Osborn, John Bayley, Joseph Sandy, Jeremiah Finney, Henry Hamton, John Thurston, Richard Hammon, William Brenton, Watching Atherton, John Wilson, William Throop, Maj. Robert Thompson, Thomas Bletsoe, Samuel Cobbett, John Birge, Richard White.

## EFFORTS TO SETTLE A GOSPEL MINISTRY.

The Proprietors of Bristol and their associates were fully imbued with the spirit of the Puritan and Pilgrim Commonwealths, and took early measures to secure an able Gospel Ministry. During the first year of the settlement they obtained the services of the REV. BENJAMIN WOODBRIDGE,* who removed

---

*Mr. Woodbridge was a son of the REV. JOHN WOODBRIDGE, who was the first pastor of the first Church at Andover, Mass., and a grandson of the REV. JOHN WOODBRIDGE, who was a distinguished dissenting minister of Stanton, Wiltshire, England.

His mother was a daughter of the HON. THOMAS DUDLEY, married in 1641. His grandmother was a daughter of the REV. ROBERT PARKER, who, by his writings, is well known to have been a strong friend and advocate of non-conformity.

The father, born about the year 1613, was sent to Oxford to be educated, but refusing to take the oath of conformity, he was obliged to leave the University, and pursued his studies privately. In 1634 he came to this country with his uncle, the Rev. Thomas Parker. In 1641 he married and settled at Andover. Upon the invitation of his friends in England, he returned there in 1647. In 1662, being ejected by the Bartholomew Act, he again came to this country and became an assistant to Mr. Parker. Subsequently he was a magistrate of the Colony. He lived to see three of his sons, John, Benjamin and Timothy, in the Ministry, and four of his grandsons preparing for it. He died 1695, March 17, in the eighty-second year of his age. "The piety," says his biographer, "which he imbibed in his childhood increased with his years. He possessed a wonderful command of his passions, and afflictions and

here with his family and continued his labors about six years. At the first, beyond the provision of a "house to live in" and wood sufficient for his family's use for one year, there was no fixed salary, but various amounts were rated at different times, probably according to the supposed need of his family and the ability of the town. A house, owned by Nathaniel Byfield, and situated on Byfield street, near the present residence of Hon. I. F. Williams, was hired by the town for Mr. Woodridge's residence, and the lower south room of the same for Sabbath services and other meetings, for which Mr. Byfield received £10 rent per year.

November 29, 1684, it was voted "that Mr. Woodbridge's salary for this year be made up to Eighty pounds as Money,—and for the next year to be made up Ninety pounds as Money,—and for the year 1686 to be made up as a Hundred pounds as Money, and the sum for each year to be yearly made up, discounting of each year so much as shall be contributed by strangers; and the Hundred per annum to continue till the time that, by agreement of the Court of Plymouth, the Town is to pay towards the Colony charge, and then to come to such further settlement

---

losses did not shake his peace. Just before his death he refused a glass of wine which was offered him, saying, I am going where I shall have better."

Mr. Woodbridge was ordained over "the Presbyterian party" in Windsor, Conn., 1670, March 18, and after a Ministry of about ten years came to Bristol.

with Mr. Woodbridge as may be according to the ability of the Town, whether it be more or less. And for the raising of the sum yearly, for Mr. Woodbridge, it is to be by contribution, if what they contribute be not less than their proportion according to such rules as are hereafter set down, and such as contribute short, or not at all, to be Rated by the Selectmen, and gathered by the Constable each year."

This vote met with considerable opposition in the town, and the ninth of December following was rescinded, and the following proposal of Mr. Woodbridge was adopted, viz.: "I do propose that from the twenty-fifth day of April next, and so onward during my continuance, I will take up with a free and weekly contribution. Provided, if it doth not amount to sixty pounds per annum, the Town forthwith to make it up, and if ever it come to above an Hundred per annum, the overplus to be at their disposal."

The labors of Mr. Woodbridge were not sufficiently acceptable to some of the leading citizens to favor his settlement, although no opposition was made to employing his services temporarily. This state of things was unfortunate, both for Mr. Woodbridge, who desired a permanent settlement, and for the town, which needed a settled Minister and a regularly organized Church. At length the subject was brought before the Town at a meeting, 1686, May 17, when it was propounded whether any persons were against the settling of Mr. Woodbridge. Eleven persons voted against his settlement, and between twenty and thirty voted in his favor.

About this time the following letter was addressed "to the Rever'd Mr. James Allen, Mr. Increase Mather, and Mr. Samuel Willard in Boston.*

"BRISTOL, the 11th May, 1686.

GENTLEMEN:—There is a few lines subscribed by myselfe & some others that I suppose you will have the perusal of, & though there is not oppertunity fully to lay things before you, yet I know not but without coming to perticulers you may see reason not to encourage Mr. Woodbridge staying with us. I am satisfied that he is not like to have a quiet & peaceable settlement; nay, those that are estimated by him to be his greatest friends & most desire his settling, yet own they doe not see any probability of it. You may hear somewhat of our motions by Mr. Byfield, but there is more to be said that probable he will mind, but if put upon proofs by Mr. Woodbridges not owning or denying wee must desire time not exspecting this would be the manner or the season of issueing but rather an oppertunity of advising. That I may a little give you the state of some things with us please consider

That here in this town 14 [or 15] men that have been members of other churches, Mr. Woodbridge instead of getting more Interest in these hath brought it to that now but 3 that I can perceive can act for his settling.

Among them that are the Proprietors soe called being about 18 in number, though they are not willing to vote him out of town, yet I cannot perceive as things are circumstanced that there is above 5 or 6 that act for his settling.

Take the Town as a Town & I know not whether it will not be good to see who they be & how many that are for recalling & further encourageing him, both which I per-

*Mass. Hist. Coll., VIII., 4th Series, 651.

ceive he exspects. For Mr. Woodbridges first call which he hath built upon ever since was when we were not a Town & were not a Third so many concerned as now are.

Our designe in the paper we have some of us subscribed & sent. is not to give an account of how many in the Town are dissatisfyed, but that you may see that many of them who are principally exspected to act in Church matters are not satisfyed & though there be but 7 of the 14 I mention above have subscribed, yet I can make out what I there write to be true.

It is exspected that there should be a Town meeting, though those Mr. Woodbridge reckoned when he went away should promote it have been cold in it since, but they have rec'd a note from Mr. Woodbridge that surely will put them that are desirous of his returning to be upon action & it will be with lesse offence for them that are for him to appear then for others that are not satisfyed to act against him. It hath been a great wrong for Mr. Woodbridg he hath allways reckoned his Interest greater than it is. Some there are that are sincerely for him no doubt; but if he will make it his own act to leave us I doubt not but matters with us would quickly be quieted, more than the charge of making Mr. Woodbridg satisfaction for what he hath laid out; if he demand, it will render the thing grievous to some. But if wee part I am for doing all things wee are capable of that can rationally be required of us. For my own perticuler I can truly say I never have managed any perticuler controversie with him. I endeavored his settlement & promoted his Interest & boare with many discouragements as long as I thought I ought or could doe with a good conscience. It was allways my unhappiness, that whatever I managed, really designing his benefit, other constructions were made of it by him; but that I easyly gott over & thought he should act for himself, or they for him that he thought could doe it more to his satisfaction. I have slited or took little notice of many affronts I have mett with, but some word he hath said of late that I have heard him speake, some own others & that I believe I can make out the rest, that I must needs say I take not well from him. How farr of late he hath been guilty in spreading a false report of me in matters that have been much to my damidg & discredit, might be made out if need were. That he should charge me with haveing designs as deep as the bottomless pitt; That he should charge mee not only that my designs tended to it, but that my design was to ruin this town, whereas on the contrary it sufficiently appears I have rather adventured the undoing of myselfe for the good of the Town; That he should charge me that because I was sometimes ready to justifye my sincerity in all our late motions respecting him, & that I had peace in my conscience, lett others charge me how they would, That he believed I had some secret inward guilt lay on mee that made me speake soe much of my peace in these matters; & then at a Town Meeting, where there was a peaceable issue in ade of some affairs of the Town which it is said he is troubled at, that he should say he questioned whether I had anything to do to vote there. These & other such charges & reflections I never deserved from him, or had he reason for, but these are things that I have not had account of or heard but a little while & therefore not in the least to be reckoned as any part of the ground of my former unsatisfyedness with him. To goe about to give an account of the occasions & reasons of my dissatisfaction & by what degrees it came to that heighth that now it is, would be a larger taske than I can now goe about; but if what Mr. Byfield hath to offer be no ground I doubt not but I shall be able to say that & more when there is oppertunity.

These lines are writt in haste. Be pleased to put a candid construction thereon. I thanke God I hope I can truely say I would be found doeing of that which is my duty, could easyly passe by personal injurys. It is not the matter of maintenance or anything of any such nature, but an assured & I think well grounded confidence that his settling here is not like to be with love & peace & any competent satisfaction to those that are principally aimed at for carrying on church affairs. If he come again there is no hopes of settling church affairs that I foresee; if it be, it will be in some strange and unusual way, & if there be not a settlement of these matters according to the practice of other Churches what sober men that are among us that can will endeavor to remove from us, & we expect no sober men to come to us & our place indeed will be outdone. I have mett with several losses & disappointments of late & unexpected dealings from some men, but I reckon this not among the least of my troubles. I hope God will doe me good by all. I should earnestly desire & gladly accept a few lines from you to advise me in anything you thinke necessary. Shall not add but my service & hearty respects to each of you, desiring your prayers for mee, that I may be kept in this hour of temptation & that I may be directed in my duty & found doeing those things that may be for the glory of God and the best good of this place.

Your friend & servant,

JOHN WALLEY."

The following is a copy of the document referred to by Mr. Walley and addressed to the same persons, at the same date or a little before.*

[This letter, with the exception of the signatures of the other persons whose names are attached, is in the hand-writing of Mr. Walley.]

" Whereas God who setteth the bounds of the habitations of the children of men; hath in his sovereign wisdome disposed soe many of us to this place as he hath, wee

*Mass. Hist. Coll., VIII., 4th series, 695.

do desire to be found doeing those things in our several places & capacities that may be for the glory of His name, the promoting the Interest & Kingdome of Jesus Christ & to be laying of such foundations as might be for the good of ourselves & our Children after us & as it is our duty soe it hath been our earnest desire that we might enjoy not onely the preaching of the word, but other the ordinances of Jesus Christ & although from time to time wee have been in the use of means in order thereunto (yet to our griefe) we find things more & more unlikely for obtaining the same & our motions therein have been hindered, as wee thinke by him who should have most encouraged the same. The Rev'd Mr. Woodbridge, in his paper he left with the Town speaks of his return, if it might be with peace, incouragement and joynt concurrence, neither of which wee thinke he will procure & when we have been discoursing about gathering a church in this place he hath not been willing to promote the same in any way, without he could see some certainty of his being settled & called to office therein. And wee the subscribers, having had oppertunity to take notice of Mr. Woobdridge his methods & designs among us, have reason to think his settlement here will not be for the glory of God, his good, nor ours; he having had many oppertunities wherein to have had a competent comfortable & quiet settlement among us & he never having embraced the same & being he would not be persuaded to fall in therewith, makes us ready to think that his worke will be rather in some other place than here & that he is not the man that God intends to doe us good by. And if he should be voated in as a minister by a major part of the Town (which we question) or imposed upon us by others we must beare it and desire we may as becomes Christians; but to be active for his settlement & especially to have any hand in calling him to office amongst us wee must be excused in. It is our griefe that things fall out soe among us. Wee are troubled for him as well as for ourselves, & doe solemnly declare it is not out of any prejudice to his person or any perticular interest or controversie of our own, but the keeping of a good conscience in the discharg of our duty wee owe to God, to the Town, to ourselves & one to another; & anything wee can doe for him, that wee may & ought to doe, wee would not be wanting in, & wee do believe that if he would make it his own act to leave us, it would be the readyest way to settle us, & we trust God will provide for us. To give the reasons of our discouragements wee have not now time for, but if any necessity lyes upon it wee think wee should have time, & if the decision of matters is to be by a Council wee thinke it ought to be upon the place, & then will be best opportunity to understand the state of things with us. In the meane time your counsel & advice to us & prayers for us is earnestly desired by your servants to our power.

John Carey,
Hugh Woodbury,
Nathaniel Reynells,
Nathaniel Bosworth,
John Walley,
Nathaniel Byfield.

A few weeks later another letter respecting this subject was addressed "To the Reverend Mr. Increase Mather, Teacher of the Second Church of Christ in Boston. To be communicated to the Church."* The following is a copy of this letter:

"Honored, Reverend & Beloved in our Lord Jesus,—It is, we doubt not, by the Churches and faithfull in Christ sadly observed, that there are verie uncomfortable disagreements among us in this Place, which have an Evill & perilous tendency.

---

*Mass. Hist. Coll., VIII., 654.

And (with griefe wee speake it) of such a Nature they are, and such an influence they have that our peace is much impaired, the worke of Christ Obstructed, our quiet settlement in a way of Church Order and Gospell fellowship for the present wholly hindered and the name of God much dishonored.

And although some of us (of God's abundant Grace, and not for any worth in us) have sometimes tasted the Good of Communion with God in His ordinances, which, if our hearts deceive us not, leaves such an impression upon our spirits that we would be willing to Deny ourselves to the uttermost; Rather than become Guiltye of not doing what God Requires of us, to our severall abillityes & in our severall capacityes for the enjoyment thereof, and the settling of a Gospel Church and Ministrie here in a way of peace and order: yet soo it hath pleased God to denye His Presence and Blessing with our endeavours for some years past, that our essays hitherto have bin successles, and our condition at this time is very deplorable. We do therefore Earnestly Request yourselves in our present difficultie to affoard us your helpe by your Elders and Messengers upon the third Wednesday of July next, that being here at that time Assembled they may fully hear & Consider our Case, and give us the Counsell & Advice in the Lord, who, we hope will open our hearts to Receive it; in order whereunto we intreate your prayers, that we may see, & be humbled for our sins, which have been a provocation to God & that the Lord will Graciously be reconciled to us & accept us in the Lord Jesus, in whom we are

Your Assured friends to serve you,

John Walley,
Nathal. Byfield.
Nathaniel Reynells,
Nathaniel Bosworth,
John Cary,
Hugh Woodbury.

Bristoll, June 28th, 1686.
For ourselves & in the behalfe of sundry others."

We have found no record of the Council thus called. It seems highly probable that it resulted in the withdrawal of Mr. Woodbridge by his own act, and the restoration of peace.*

---

*He was not long after settled in Kittery, Me. In 1691 he resided in Portsmouth, N. H. In 1698 he was living in Charlestown, Mass., and was employed by the town of Medford to preach for six months, provision being made for conveyance from his home to Medford every Saturday, and return every Monday. His preaching was so generally acceptable that movements were made to give him a call, but matters were not hastened, and, at length, difficulties arose which prevented his settlement. He was, however, anxious to settle, and persisted in acting as the town's minister, contrary to the advice of a Council of Clergymen and Elders from Boston; and, in spite of votes of the town in 1704, "that what they had done about Mr. W.'s settlement be null and void," and in 1705, "that they would not proceed to settle Mr. W. as their minister." With a few earnest friends he attempted to gather a church "contrary to the advice of the Elders in the neighborhood, without advice or respect of the inhabitants of the town, and without the countenance and concurrence of the neighboring churches." This highly irregular attempt was met by an earnest protest from the town. Appeals were then made to the "General Sessions of Peace," at Charlestown, and to "Gov. Dudley and his Council," both of which were decided adversely to the claims and course of Mr. W. Finally, the case was referred to a Council of Churches who censured both parties, and advised the quiet withdrawal of Mr. W. The advice was not followed. however, and Mr. W. continued to preach until his death, 1710, January 15, after a residence of nearly ten years, aged sixty-five years; and on the same day, with commendable

## ERECTION OF A HOUSE OF WORSHIP.

The first public religious service in Bristol was in the dwelling house of DEACON NATHANIEL BOSWORTH, a building still standing, occupied as the residence of J. DEW. PERRY, ESQ. Afterwards Sabbath services were held in COLONEL BYFIELD'S house, Byfield street, to which reference has previously been made. These arrangements were temporary, to continue only until such time as the inhabitants could build a House of Worship.

In the "Grand Articles" of agreement between the Proprietors and those to whom they made grants of land and other privileges, it was stipulated among other things, "that every one shall and will, according to his estate, pay his proportion of the charge for the erecting and building of the Meeting House and Minister's House and accommodations thereunto, when and at such time as those that have the major part proprietary in said land shall nominate and appoint."

October 24th, 1683, at a Town meeting, two hundred and fifty pounds were ordered to be raised, to defray the expense of building a Meeting House; and JOHN WALLEY, NATHANIEL BYFIELD, BENJAMIN CHURCH, JOHN CARY and JOHN ROGERS were ap-

---

promptitude and just liberality, the town voted ten pounds to defray the expenses of his funeral,—an act which proves that they would not let the sun go down upon their animosity.—*Brooks' Hist. of Medford*, 203–208.

pointed a committee to superintend its erection. Measures were promptly taken to carry out this vote. A plan of house was soon adopted, and the work commenced. Citizens who could be well employed on the building were so employed and the value of their labor allowed on their taxes. The timbers were cut from the Common, near by, and with united zeal and courage the work progressed until a spacious and well constructed Sanctuary stood before them to the joy of their hearts, a monument of their self-denying interest in the Cause of the Redeemer. This House was erected on the spot where now stands the State Court House. We find no record of its exact dimensions, but tradition describes it as "spacious; square in its form like the Apocalyptic City; clapboarded inside and out; having double galleries one above the other; with a cap-roof, surmounted in the centre with a cupola and bell, from which a rope was suspended directly beneath, by which 'GOODY CORPS,' the sexton's widow, used to ring the people to church for three pounds per year, as her lamented husband had done ere he died;" over the preacher's head, a dormer window, and on all sides double rows of windows for the ingress of light; and the floor, divided into square pews with oaken doors, "through the rounds of which the children used to peep at each other when the people rose for prayer and praise." These pews were constructed from time to time by the citizens as they were able, by leave of the town, and several years elapsed before the floor was all covered.

Considering the pecuniary circumstances of the people, this effort was a remarkable instance of self-sacrifice and consecration to the higher interests of religion. They were few in number, feeble in resources, and had scarcely sheltered their families in their humble dwellings, when they gave their best energies to building a habitation of God. At a sacrifice of toil and money, of which we in our comparative abundance can have little conception, they secured for themselves this Religious Home, and with glad songs of praise dedicated it to the worship ot Almighty God. We may smile at the severe simplicity of style, devoid of architectural beauty; unprotected in winter by warming apparatus, and in summer offering literally to the swallow a place to build her nest and lay her young upon its unceiled arches; its family pews square and roomy; and its high pulpit, surmounted with pendent sounding board, seeming ready to fall and crush the man of God beneath its weight, as he discoursed of the awful wrath of God towards impenitent sinners; yet we cherish the most tender and hallowed associations clustering around this first Sanctuary of the fathers in the wilderness.

This quaint building, laboriously erected by the pioneers of our civilization, and dedicated to the worship of Almighty God, was the only Sanctuary in town for nearly forty years, and the home of the first church for a round century. Here our pious ancestry sat and listened to messages of Divine Truth and salvation, raised their hearts in prayer and praise to

God, and received nourishment of spiritual life. Here were they trained for the kingdom of glory, and to-day their notes of praise respond to angelic harps around the throne of God in heaven. Although of the people who once lived on earth and worshipped here not one remains, and of the people now living not one ever saw this House of God, we cherish tender thoughts of the past, and preserve with veneration the door of the pastor's pew, the only remaining relic of the Sanctuary where our fathers worshipped God for one hundred years.

### ORGANIZATION OF THE CHURCH.

Not long after the retirement of Mr. Woodbridge, the Rev. Samuel Lee, D. D., an English dissenting Clergyman, celebrated among his contemporaries as a man of profound learning and ardent piety, arrived in Boston, and was cordially received by his Brethren and the Churches. Great interest had been awakened for the cause of Christ in Bristol, which seemed to suffer from the divisions that had sprung up under the Ministry of Mr. Woodbridge. Friends in Boston felt that it was of the highest importance that a man of commanding abilities and established reputation for soundness in the faith and wisdom should at once occupy this field, around whom the people might rally in union, and under whose direction a Church of Christ might be founded. At their suggestion he visited Bristol, and at once the hearts of the people went out to him as being sent of God, and the conviction became almost universal that he was the man for whose coming they had prayed, suffered and waited.

Measures were promptly taken to secure his settlement. The Town Records, 1686, November 23, give the following account of his enthusiastic reception by the people, who went from the Town Meeting in a body to enforce their call by the magnetism of their presence.

"Then voted and agreed by a full vote and unanimous consent, to call the Rev. Samuel Lee to the work of the ministry in this town, which was accordingly done by the whole that were present at the Town Meeting. waiting on him at Mr. Byfield's, where one appointed manifested their invitation to him and he took it into consideration."

Sixty pounds per year was voted by the town for his salary, and fifty pounds towards building him a house.* The lands for the Ministry set apart by the Proprietors in the settlement of the town were also voted him. This call he accepted, and began his labors 1687, April 10.

---

*As speedily as practicable, a spacious mansion, built in the old English style and, it is said, by far the most elegant dwelling in town, was erected on the east side of Thames street, which was then the shore of the harbor. This house was afterwards owned by JEREMIAH FINNEY, descended by inheritance to his son, JOSIAH FINNEY, and was the birthplace of all his children. In it was born the wife of the late WILLIAM DEWOLF, ESQ., who, with her sister MARTHA, occupied in their early days the sacred study chamber where the man of God studied, wrote and prayed

The third day of May following was observed as a day of fasting and prayer, in the midst of which sacred season the Church was organized in due form by the mutual consent of eight fathers of the town. The following is a copy of the record of these events taken from the earliest records of the Church, in the almost illegible hand of Deacon John Carey, whose name heads the page.

"In the year 1687, it pleased God to bringe that reverend Mr. Lee to Bristol, and [it was (?)] on visit to se the plac[e] and preach to the peopell. Ther was a joynt voat of the town for his taking charg heer to preach the gospell, and in order of settlinge the plac[e] in gospell order; which after some short spac[e] came with his wife and family to settel heer."

"The 10th of April he begins with us, in order thereunto '87. * * * * * *

"May the third was the church gathered by the mutual consent and agreement of thos[e] persons mentioned.

MAJOR JOHN WALLEY, CAPTAIN NATHANIEL BYFIELD, CAPTAIN BENJAMIN CHURCH, NATHANIEL REYNOLDS, JOHN CAREY, HUGH WOODBURY, GOODMAN THROUP, NATHANIEL BOSWORTH whom they elected DEACON."

---

for his beloved people. The two eldest of Mr. DeWolf's children were also born here. For many years this house was known as "The Old Bay State," we know not why, unless it may be because it was so redolent with the associations of Puritan ideas, which are the glory of Massachusetts. The only relic of it now remaining is a pane of glass inscribed with the name MARTHA FINNEY, in the possession of a descendant of the family.

The 8th of May '87 was the first sacrament in Bristol: Con.-0-4-3 the Contribution-0-11-2.

Major Walley's daughter Elizabeth that day baptized, Nathaniel Reynolds his sone Benjamin baptized.—The two first in that Church."

Thus was the First Church gathered in Bristol, the first of the Congregational order within the present limits of Rhode Island.* At the organization, and for many years afterwards, the Church was known as "THE CHURCH OF CHRIST IN BRISTOL." After the incorporation of the Catholic Congregational Society in 1784, the Church was, by common consent, called "THE CATHOLIC CONGREGATIONAL CHURCH." By this name it was known until, in order to hold and protect Charitable funds entrusted to its care, it was incorporated by act of the General Assembly in 1869, under the title "THE FIRST CONGREGATIONAL CHURCH IN BRISTOL." This is our present name and appropriate designation, though we be no less a simple "Church of Christ" than when we began, and are no less "Catholic" in our fellowship with all who love our Lord in sincerity, and strive to do his will.

Our Church life began in prayer to God, who graciously directed those sturdy pioneers as they bowed

---

*The Church at East Providence is older, but its members are from both East Providence and Seekonk, Mass., and it has always been identified in Conference relations with the Massachusetts Churches. The Church in Barrington has also been claimed as being organized at an earlier date, but it is stated in Bicknell's History, p. 180, "that no distinct Church with a thorough Congregational polity was established until after the year 1711, and prior to 1718."

before Him. Firmly, therefore, were the foundations of our spiritual edifice laid, and though the storms of earth have beaten against it, all these years it has stood, because it was founded upon a rock.

## BIOGRAPHICAL NOTES OF THE EARLY MEMBERS.

The constituent members of the Church were all men of excellent character and leading influence in the town, and some of them were also prominent actors in Colonial affairs, and held stations of honor which gave them a national reputation.

JOHN WALLEY, the first on the list of members, one of the four original proprietors of the town, was highly respected and honored with various offices which he discharged with marked ability and fidelity. In all efforts for the civil, social, moral and religious welfare of the community he was among the foremost of the citizens, and favored the most liberal provisions for these ends. He loved the Church of Christ with singular devotion, and it was a great grief to him that the organization of the Church in Bristol was so long delayed. He was ever the warm friend and hearty supporter of the Gospel Ministry, and, while he conscientiously opposed the settlement of Mr. Woodbridge, and, perhaps more than any other man, was instrumental in his removal, he yet rejoiced in all the good he accomplished, and was among the readiest to give him liberal pecuniary support as long as he remained.

Nor were the public services of Mr. Walley confined to Bristol. He was well known throughout

New England, and especially in Boston, where he had lived and engaged successfully and honorably in mercantile pursuits, his valuable public labors were in frequent call. He was, for a season, Judge of the Superior Court, and a member of the Governor's Council. In 1690 he had command of the land forces in the expedition of Sir William Phipps, against Canada, of which he published a journal which is preserved in Hutchinson's history. Although this expedition was unsuccessful, it involved much heroic self-sacrifice and reflected honor both upon the men and their commanding officer.

Mr. Walley was a son of the Rev. Thomas Walley, of London, who was at one time Rector of St. Mary's White Chapel, and said to be a man of great esteem; who was one of the eight ministers who came from London in the "Society," Captain Pierce, arriving in Boston, 1663, May 24, and who died on Sunday, 1678, March 24, aged sixty-one years.

He came before his father and settled in Boston, whence he removed to Bristol.

His residence in this town was in the rear of State street, and his dwelling, substantially built after the style of those early times, is still standing and known as "the Walley house." His family consisted of wife and three children, two daughters and a son born here.

His daughter Sarah married Charles Chauncy, of Boston, and was the mother of a son of the same name, who became "one of the most distinguished divines on our side of the ocean," the junior Pastor of the Old South Church, referred to in the following notices of Mr. Byfield and family.

On the second of March, 1692, he was left a sorrowful widower by the decease of his loving and dutiful wife, the sharer of his joys and burdens, who departed in the triumphs of Christian faith. In the latter part of his life he returned to Boston, where he died in calmness and humble reliance upon the Great Redeemer for mercy, 1712, January 11th, in the sixty-ninth year of his age.

"The high trusts imposed by his country," says his Biographer, "were discharged with ability and fidelity. To his wisdom as a Counsellor and his impartiality as a Judge, he added an uncommon sweetness and candor of spirit and the various virtues of the Christian. His faith was justified by his integrity, his works of piety and charity."

Nathaniel Byfield was the son of the Rev. Richard Byfield, "the laborious faithful pastor of Long Ditton in Surrey, England, who was one of the oldest of the ejected ministers in that county; who afterwards retired to Montlack, where he usually preached twice every Lord's day in his own family, and did so the very Lord's day before his death, in 1664, aged sixty-seven years;" who is described as "a man of great piety, zeal and exemplary holiness of conversation;" who was one of the distinguished Westminster Assembly, that prepared that admirable compendium of Orthodox Faith, known as "the Shorter Catechism." His mother was a sister of Bishop Juxon, a noted family in England. He was the youngest of twenty-one children, and one of the sixteen that sometimes attended their pious parents to the place of public worship. He was born in 1653; arrived at Boston in 1674, and conceiving a love to this country resolved to settle here. Accordingly, he married the following year Miss DEBORAH CLARKE, and commenced business as a merchant in Boston. In this he was eminently successful, accumulating considerable property, and, at the close of Philip's war, invested a portion of his wealth in the purchase of this township. Here he became an early settler, casting in his lot with the pioneers of the wilderness, sharing with them the toils and hardships of laying the foundations of a new and well regulated community. He continued a citizen of this town forty-four years, and his influence was great in all civil and ecclesiastical affairs. His residence was on the beautiful peninsula known as Pappoosquaws Point, west of the town, and his farm embraced nearly all of the peninsula.* Here was his family tomb, prepared by himself, located on the estate of the late William D'Wolf, Esq., whose remains are traced to this day, in which were buried members of his family who deceased during his residence in

*It has been generally supposed that his dwelling house stood on the spot where Deacon William Manchester now resides, but recent investigations lead to the belief that the venerable mansion now occupied by the heirs of the late Mrs. Sarah Herreshoff, was built originally by Colonel Byfield and occupied as his residence.

Bristol. Within the recollection of persons now living, the name of "PRISCILLA" and a part of "BYFIELD," were distinctly traced upon the head-stone

He was also a large real estate owner in the compact part of the town. He had five children born here by his wife DEBORAH, three of whom died young. The other two lived to be married, the youngest to the HON. LIEUTENANT GOVERNOR TAYLOR, of Massachusetts, who soon after died without issue; the other to EDWARD LYDE, ESQ., by whom she had five children, three of whom grew up and left descendants.

MR. BYFIELD was thrifty in his habits, catholic in spirit, and generous in his benefactions, giving away systematically and cheerfully a portion of his income, amounting often to several hundred pounds yearly. One instance of his charities mentioned as worthy of special remembrance for the good it accomplished, was the publishing and gratuitously distributing an edition of ten thousand copies of the Assembly's Shorter Catechism. He was always a faithful and efficient friend of Education and Religion, and a liberal supporter of the Gospel Ministry. To his wisdom, foresight and liberality are we chiefly indebted for our broad and regular streets, our large and beauful Common, and especially *the school lands which were chiefly his own generous gift to the town, the income from which have been a material help to the cause of education here and a perpetual public charity.* Two cups of our Communion Service of solid silver are inscribed as "the gift of Nathaniel Byfield,

1693." Many other tokens of his interest in and liberal aid of the Church and Ministry here are held in remembrance with us to this day.

Nor was his large generosity confined to the limits of Bristol. His eminent abilities, natural and acquired, fitted him for a high position in affairs of State, and he cheerfully gave his services to the various offices, both civil and military, to which he was called by the suffrages of his fellow citizens as well as by royal appointment. Few have passed through a greater variety of scenes in public life. "In the field he quickly arrived to one of the highest places of power. In the State he was honored with many betrustments; was in commission for the Peace and Judge of Probate; was several times chosen Speaker in the Honorable House of Representatives; sat chief thirty-eight years in the Court of General Sessions of the Peace and Common Pleas for the county of Bristol, as afterwards he did two years for the county of Suffolk; was one of His Majesty's Council for the province of Massachusetts Bay, a great number of years; and had the honor of receiving five several commissions for Judge of the Vice Admiralty from three crowned heads; from King Willliam, in 1697; from Queen Anne, in the years 1702, 1703 and 1709, and from King George the Second in 1728." Being well informed for the exercise of authority, his very looks inspiring respect, loving order and possessed of a fine elocution, sincerely devoted to the interests of the community, he discharged all these trusts to popular acceptance.

His name throughout New England was a household word; and one of the towns of Massachusetts, although he had no special connection with its history, honored itself and paid him the homage of its respect by taking his name which it holds to the present day.

The wisdom and justice of Mr. Byfield's acts as a Civil Judge, are apparent from the remarkable fact that in no case were his decisions ever reversed on appeal to higher powers. It is still more interesting to note his freedom from those superstitious prejudices which blinded even some of the best men of his time, and which led to the cruel proceedings in the matter of "the Salem Witchcraft" that are a dark blot on the page of history. Those proceedings he had the courage to oppose and condemn; and had his counsels been followed, no innocent person would have suffered death as a witch.

He did not escape the common lot of public men to suffer unjust aspersion and severe criticisms from political rivals in his own time, and from the detractions of prejudiced or ill-informed historians who came after him; but well authenticated facts give him a highly honorable name.

NATHANIEL BYFIELD surely made his mark, and the footprints of his influence will be traced to the end of time. With all his grand and noble works of life, he had a steady and unshaken faith in the truths of the Gospel, and died in the lively hope of the glorious Redeemer. In 1724, on account of his advanced age, he returned with his family to Boston, where he closed his long and useful life 1733, June 6th, in the eightieth year of his age. The sermon preached at his funeral by his pastor in Boston, Rev. Charles Chauncy, D. D., and afterwards published, was from the text John 1:42: *Jesus saw Nathaniel coming to him and saith of him, behold an Israelite indeed in whom is no guile;* A very clear and forcible presentation of the beauty and worth of "a guileless character;" at the close of which it is applied to Mr. Byfield in these words, viz.:

"I have no need to insert here, not doubting your thot's were upon *our* Nathaniel while I was representing the character in the text; the application was so easie and obvious; and I would hope unexceptionably: having carefully avoided saying anything but what I thot in justice belonged to him."

An extract from the "Weekly News Letter," of June 14, 1733, appended to the published discourse, mentions, with other facts that are embodied in the foregoing sketch, the following:

"On the 6th of this instant, between the hours of 1 and 2 in the morning, died at his house here, after about a month's languishment, the Honourable Nathaniel Byfield, Esq., in the 80th year of his age: Having long been a great ornament both of our Church and State. * *

"For his character, justice to his memory requires it should be said—He was greatly valued and honored by those acquainted with him, for his superior genius and abilities; his great natural courage, Vigor and Activity; his plain, unaffected, cheerful and instructive way of conversation; his catholic spirit; his real Integrity, and unquestionable faithfulness and Honesty; his zeal against sin, and to maintain public peace and good order; his first regard to the worship of God, and constant and devout and exemplary attendance on it both in Public and private, and in one word his love to the Ministry, the Churches and Civil and Religious interests of this people: All which being united in the same person and in an eminent degree, as it rendered his life an extensive blessing, so his Death just matter for lamentation.

He lived with the wife of his youth till 1717, upwards of forty years; and the following year married MRS. SARAH LEVERETT, youngest daughter to the HONORABLE GOVERNOR LEVERETT, with whom he lived till 1730: when he was again left a sorrowful widower. He died with great inward peace and serenity of soul: and was honorably interred last Monday—a funeral prayer being first made by the elder Pastor of the Old Church to whose Communion he belong'd. He has left his grandson BYFIELD LYDE, ESQ.; (son-in-law to his excellency GOVERNOR BELCHER) Heir to the bulk of his Estate."

The last will of Mr. Byfield, dated 1732, December 6th, shows that he had large real estate in Boston, including mansion house, coach house, stable, cow house and two gardens joining; also, rope walk, ware house, wharf and flats; also, other tenement houses, stores, etc., and lands covering a large portion of Fort Hill, and various sites from Beacon street west and north to Cambridge street, now among the most valuable in the city; also large estate in several New England towns, together with extensive tracts of land of several thousand acres in Maine and Vermont. His Christian character is manifest in the provisions of this Will, both the reverent expression of faith towards God, and bequests of charity, together with an equitable division of property among his heirs after the full payment of all debts and other bequests. It was his principle and practice to give largely *in life* to religious and charitable objects, and he expected the heirs of his estate to follow his example in this respect; accordingly there were no large charitable bequests made in this Will, yet as a token of personal affection and respect for their office, he bequeathed gifts to "all and every" Minister of Christ, of every denomination, in Boston, to the President and professors in Cambridge, and additional bequests to his "dear pastors," FOXCROFT and CHAUNCY, of the Old South Church. His servants were remembered with Christian affection and counsel, and *freedom*, with ample provisions to secure the enjoyment of the same, was given to a favorite servant to take effect six months after his decease.

Mr. Byfield was buried in the "Granary Burial Ground," near Park street Church. The tombstone has inscribed the Byfield Coat of Arms, with the name LYDE cut on the shield. The stone which marked Mr. Byfield's grave has long since disappeared, and is supposed either to be destroyed or, in the changes made in the tomb, to be concealed from view. The following epitaph, the production of REV. MATHER BYLES, was inscribed:

"BYFIELD beneath in peaceful slumber lies;
BYFIELD the good, the active and the wise;
His manly frame contained an equal mind;
Faithful to God, and generous to mankind;

High in his country's Honors long he stood,
Succored distress and gave the hungry food;
In justice steady, in devotion warm,
A loyal subject, and Patriot firm;
Through every age his dauntless soul was tried:
Great while he lived, but greater when he died."

Mrs. Deborah Byfield, the wife of his youth and companion for about forty years, was the daughter of Captain Thomas Clarke, of Boston. She united with the Church in Bristol, soon after its organization, and tradition says, was one of the most valuable and useful of the female members, a fit associate and help-meet of her worthy husband. We regret that there are no records or materials from which a more extended notice can be given. As her decease occurred in 1717, several years before his return to Boston, it is supposed that she was buried here in the Family Tomb on his farm; but as her death is not recorded in the town books, it is possible that she died and was buried among her family friends in Boston.

Mrs. Sarah Byfield, the beloved consort of his riper years, who died in Boston, 1730, December 21, was buried in the Burial Ground where his remains were afterwards placed by her side. The Weekly News Letter, No. 1405, of date December 29, 1730, gives the following notice of the funeral:

"Yesterday were buried here the Remains of that truly honorable and devout Gentlewoman Mrs. Sarah Byfield amidst the affectionate Respects and lamentations of a numerous concourse. Before carrying out the Corpse a

Funeral prayer was made by one of the Pastors of the Old Church to whose communion she belonged: which tho' a custom in the country towns is a singular instance in this place, but it's wished may prove a leading example to the general practice of so christian and decent a custom. The Pall was held up by the HON. THE LATE LIEUT. GOV. DUMMER with other gentlemen of his Majesty's Council. Among the mourning Relatives went HIS EXCELLENCY GOVERNOR BELCHER, and HIS HONOUR LIEUT. GOV. TAILER, followed by a long train of persons of public distinction and private character; paying their last offices to the Dead, and uniting their sincere condolence with the living,"

On the Sabbath following her decease and burial, her pastor, the REV. CHARLES CHAUNCY, D. D., preached a discourse from the text, James 4: 14, on "Man's life considered under the similitude of a vapor," from which we make the following extracts:

"She had naturally a weak and tender Body, but a strong and noble soul; which being cultivated and enriched by a good education and great industry rendered her truly amiable and desirable, and fitted her to be a blessing in the station Providence had assigned her.

"Her temper was lively and cheerful, yet far from light and vain: being well ballast by a singular discretion. In her most pleasant hours, she was never unfit to enter upon a serious subject, and always treated it with a becoming gravity and reverence.

"She had a good taste in conversation and was exceedingly well turned for it, having a ready wit, a sprightly genius, an easy smooth way of expressing herself: and being able without stiffness or ostentation to be both entertaining and profitable.

"She was an honour to her sex, in her exemplary Deportment under all the various characters and relations of life: As a neighbor kind and pitiful: As a friend, true and hearty: As a wife tender and dutiful, engaging in her carriage: reverent and respectful: As mistress in a family, discreet in her management, neat and cleanly, tho'tful of all under her care, indulgent and compassionate to her servants, especially concerned about their souls, and frequent in teaching them the good knowledge of the Lord; in her treatment of strangers, hospitable; courteous, pleasant, observing and edifying to those that came to visit her.

"But her chief excellency and what most recommended to all that knew her was her undissembled piety. She had an habitual prevailing awe and reverence of God upon her heart, which early discovered itself and all along through the course of her life, not only in an utter abhorrence of everything that savored of irreverance but in a due treatment of those things wherein the Divine honor is nearly concerned. She loved the House and sanctified the day of God and gave her constant, devout attendance on the public worship and all Gospel ordinances; paid a singular regard to the Holy Scriptures; valued the Ministers of Religion; and had an universal regard to all good men. But above all Christ was the object of her love her faith, her hope. Him she embraced as the alone Redeemer of souls; Him she trusted with the great affair of her eternal salvation; him she loved with her whole heart; Him she made it her care to please in all things; His image she was adorned with, and the graces of His Spirit she lived in the daily exercise of; And we charitably believe she is gone to be with Christ, which is best of all."*

Benjamin Church, the third on the list of origi-

---

*For these memoranda of Mrs. Byfield, also items given in sketches of Mr. Byfield, we are indebted to a volume of Sermons in "the Prince Library," Boston, containing the two funeral discourses of Dr. Chauncy.

nal members, is a prominent name in the early Colonial history.

He was a son of RICHARD CHURCH, who came to Massachusetts in the fleet with GOV. WINTHROP; a carpenter by trade; lived at Wessagusset (Weymouth,) and Plymouth, where he was admitted a freeman in 1633; married ELIZABETH, daughter of RICHARD WARREN, in 1636; was often a member of the "Grand Enquest," and frequently chosen as a Referee; served as Sergeant in the Pequot war; helped build the first Meeting House in Plymouth about 1637; was in Charlestown in 1653; but finally settled in Hingham, where he made his will 1668, December 25th, and died two days after at Dedham, leaving nine children.

He was born at Plymouth, in 1639, and was bred to his father's trade. 1667, December 26th, he married ALICE SOUTHWORTH, grand-daughter of the distinguished wife of Gov. BRADFORD, second daughter of CONSTANT and ELIZABETH (COLLIER) SOUTHWORTH, of Duxbury, born in 1646. Their early married life was passed in Duxbury, though he temporarily resided in various parts of the Colony in the pursuit of his vocation.

Less than six months after his father's death, 1669, June 1st, he received from the Court a grant of "land att Taunton River," which William Pabodie had taken up and then surrendered, "for full satisfaction for all the right his father Richard Church, deceased, hath to land in this Collonie." He was for many years in the almost constant employ of the

Colony, on juries for the trial of both civil and criminal cases, and was the Constable of Duxbury.

In 1674, influenced by the representations of Captain John Almy, of Rhode Island, whose acquaintance he had made during a session of the Court at Plymouth, he visited the territory known then by the Indian names *Pocasset* and *Sogkonate*, now Little Compton, R. I., was pleased with it, made a purchase, settled a farm, and soon erected two buildings upon it. This farm was in the north-west part of the town, near the east passage of Narragansett Bay. He was the first Englishman that settled here, "gained a good acquaintance with the Natives, got much into their favour, and was in a little time in great esteem among them."

During the following spring, while he was diligently employed on his farm, and hoping that his good success would be inviting unto other good men to become his neighbors, the rumor of a war between the English and Natives gave check to his peaceful projects. Being informed by *Weetamoe* and some of her chief men of the inimical intentions of PHILIP, the Sachem of Mount Hope, and receiving fuller intelligence of the same at a Great Dance given by *Awashonks* Squaw Sachem of the "Sogkonate" Indians, to which she had invited him, he immediately set out for Plymouth to apprise the Authorities there and take counsel with them respecting measures to be taken in the emergency. From this time until the close of Philip's war, he was employed in the service of the Colony. Distinguished for remarkable physical vigor and activity, exposed from childhood to the perils of Indians, and understanding thoroughly their mode of warfare, he rendered most valuable services as a military leader, and to him more than to any other man belongs the honor of bringing to a victorious close that bloodiest and most terrific of the Indian wars, known as King Philip's war. Late in life he dictated to his son, THOMAS CHURCH, ESQ., a narrative of this war and of later expeditions, which was published, passed through several editions, and is still the standard history of those times. He was at the head of the party by which KING PHILIP was slain in the swamp at the foot of Mount Hope, and by his skill and bravery a few days after, ANNOWAN, the last of Philip's great war chiefs, was taken captive. His surprise and capture of this warrior has been described as "an act of heroic boldness which has no parallel in modern times." His numerous and perilous adventures with the savages in the region of Narragansett Bay and Cape Cod, read like a volume of romance. His success in these encounters inspired such confidence, that he was subsequently charged with the command of five different expeditions against the Indians in Maine, with the rank of Major and afterwards of Colonel. In consequence of his long and bloody conflict with the savage Indians, he has been unjustly represented as of a hard-hearted and cruel disposition. But he had a merciless and treacherous foe to contend with, and there remained no alternative but to meet them on their own ground and by their own acts of warfare, or suffer them to carry desolation and death in their most horrid forms through the scattered and feeble settlements of the white men. The historian of Fall River says, "In raising up such a man as BENJAMIN CHURCH for the defense of the Colonists, and in preserving his life amid the imminent perils to which he was subjected, the finger of Divine Providence was most signally manifested." Before the impartial historian this veteran of Indian warfare stands "as a man of integrity and piety, a benefactor to his country, and a friend to his race."

He was no less devout as a Christian than he was brave as a warrior. "I was ever sensible," he says, "of my own littleness and unfitness to be employed in such great services, but calling to mind that God is strong I endeavored to put all my confidence in Him, and by His almighty power was carried through every difficult action, and my desire is that His name may have all the praise." "I desire prayers that I may be enabled well to accomplish my spiritual warfare and that I may be more than conqueror through Jesus Christ's loving me." In his home especially he was the devout and consistent Christian. He regularly maintained family worship, wherein he read, and often expounded the scriptures to his household. In the observance of the Sabbath and in attending the worship and ordinances of God in the Sanctuary he was exemplary.

After the close of Philip's war he removed to this town and cast in his lot with the first settlers. He purchased largely of the original proprietors and held for many years much landed estate. He built the house known as the "Old Talbee House," still standing, near the corner of Thames and Constitution streets. He was frequently elected to offices of trust and served the town with marked fidelity and wisdom. He was public spirited and contributed with great liberality for the support of institutions of Religion and Education. He was several times chosen Deputy to represent the town at Plymouth, and in 1696 was representative at Boston. He had seven children, five sons and two daughters—several of whom were born in Bristol, and have descendants still living among us.

From Bristol he moved to Fall River and subsequently to Little Compton, where he spent his last days on his farm. As years advanced he became uncomfortably corpulent in person. Being severely wounded by a fall from his horse, he sank under it and died. He was buried with military honors in the cemetery on the Common, where the visitor today may stand over his ashes and read how highly he was revered in the significant inscription upon his tomb stone. "Here lieth interred the body of the Honorable Colonel Benjamin Church, Esq., who departed this life Jan. 17, 1717–18, in the 78th year of his age."

> High in esteem among the great he stood,
> His wisdom made him lovely, great and good.
> Though he be said to die he still survives
> Through future time his memory shall live."

JOHN CARY, fifth on the list of members, emigrated from Bridgewater, Mass., to Bristol, among the earliest settlers, and established himself as a Brewer, residing on what is known as Malt house lane, deriving its name doubtless from his business. He was the eldest son of JOHN CARY and ELIZABETH GODFREY, who came to Plymouth Colony in 1630. He had ten brothers and sisters. His father was a man of superior education and had great influence in the colony and as an officer of the Church, and, tradition says, "he taught the first Latin school in the colony, and was very pious and public spirited."

On coming to Bristol, Mr. Cary at once took a prominent position in civil and ecclesiastical affairs, and was frequently elected to offices of trust. Soon after the organization of the Church he was chosen DEACON as an associate with DEACON BOSWORTH, which office he held to the day of his death. His family consisted of his wife ABIGAIL, and eleven children, seven of whom were born previous to coming to Bristol, and four of them here. Most of these grew up from childhood in the covenant relation of baptism, and were worthy and exemplary members of the Church. Two of the sons were Deacons and the husband of one of the daughters, SAMUEL HOWLAND. He died and was buried in the ancient burying ground on the Common. An upright stone was erected to his memory bearing the following inscription:

"Remember death. Here lies ye dust of DEACON JOHN CARY, a shining pattern of piety whose spirit returned to

God that gave it July 14th, 1721, in ye 76th year of his age.

> " A man of prayer, so willing to do good,
> His highest worth, who of us understood;
> Fear God, love Christ, help souls their work to mend,
> So like this saint fit for bliss without end."

Respecting the other constituent members we have only the briefest memoranda. NATHANIEL REYNOLDS was the son of ROBERT REYNOLDS, of Watertown, Mass., in 1635, perhaps, born in England. He was by trade a shoemaker as was also his father. He lived a while in Boston, where he was admitted freeman in 1665, was a member of the Artiliery company and commanded a company in King PHILIP'S war under COLONEL CHURCH. He removed to Bristol among the first settlers and was an active and useful citizen, and an exemplary Christian. He died in the faith of the Redeemer at an advanced age, 1708, July 20.

HUGH WOODBURY was the son of WILLIAM WOODBURY, born in Salem, Mass., 1650, June 30. His wife was Mary, daughter of Thomas Dixey, and they had several children, but the name in this town has long been extinct. He was among the first who settled here and appears to have been a worthy citizen, respected and honored both in civil and ecclesiastical relations. He died 1702, April 17th, in the fifty-second year of his age.

WILLIAM THROOP, called " Goodman Throop " in the record, came from Barnstable in 1680, and was a son of WILLIAM THROOP, who came from Leyden in

1640. Tradition says he was a very pious and godly man and highly respected, as were also his children, two of whom became Deacons in the Church and filled that office for many years. He died 1704, December 4th.

NATHANIEL BOSWORTH was a son of DEACON BENJAMIN BOSWORTH and REBECCA STEVENS his wife, born in Hingham, Mass., in 1651. He first settled in Rehoboth, and removed to Bristol in 1680. His mother was killed by the Indians in the early part of King PHILIP'S war. His family were numerous and many were their descendants. He was a cooper by trade and a fisherman, and tradition says he worked hand in hand with his associate, Deacon Cary, not only in the interests of their business, but in promoting the welfare of Zion which was their chief joy. He was chosen Deacon at the organization of the Church and continued in the office until his death, 1690, August 31st, in the vigor of early manhood.

Such were the men, earnest, devoted, godly and highly esteemed, who gave the weight of their character and influence to the foundations of our beloved Zion. We wonder not that such men in the Divine Providence drew around them and left behind them many others of kindred spirit. Every decade of our history has furnished those whose names are worthy of special commendation for their faith, their integrity, their shining example of Christian character.

But not the men alone were thus worthy. Though

at the organization of the Church the fathers of the town only united, the mothers in Israel soon after joined them. In their humbler spheres they were equally faithful, and then, as in our later history and as in the almost universal history of Christ's Church in earth has been true of godly women, they contributed the largest share of christian graces to the Church life, and by far the brightest light, in its daily shining before the world.

## SAMUEL LEE, D. D., FOUNDER AND FIRST PASTOR. HIS LIFE, MINISTRY, AND PUBLISHED WORKS.

MR. LEE was a son of MR. SAMUEL LEE, a wealthy and highly respected citizen of London, and was born in the year 1625. He early in life manifested a fondness for books, which his parents were pleased to gratify, sending him to the celebrated "St. Paul's School" to pursue his studies preparatory for college. Such was his proficiency here that in 1640, at the early age of fifteen years, he entered the University of Oxford, where he took and maintained high rank as a scholar, and in 1648, received the degree of Master of Arts. He was soon after settled in a Fellowship in Wadham College, and, having been a highly successful lecturer in Great St. Helen's Church in London, he was, in 1656, appointed Proctor of the University. These offices were well sustained, and gained for him the reputation among his contemporaries of being a man of very superior learning and moral worth.

At the time of the famous "Bartholomew Act" which deprived nearly two thousand clergymen of their parishes and pecuniary support, because of their dissent from some of the prescribed forms and ceremonies of the Established Church, his sympathies were heartily with the Dissenters, although he had himself no preferment to lose. After the death of the minister of a Non-Conformist Church in Holburn, London, which took place in 1667, he was associated in the pastorate of that Church with the celebrated REV. THEOPHILUS GALE. In September, 1679, we find him settled at Bignal near Bicester, in Oxfordshire, and he was afterwards, for several years, the Minister of an Independent Church, at Newington Green, near Bishopgate, in London.

After these years of distinguished service in the Ministry of Non-Conforming Churches, he was urged by BISHOP WILKINS to accept a living in the Established Church, and was strongly advised thereto by many of his friends. But his dissent from the ceremonies and usages of that Church was conscientious and hearty, and while he was liberal to concede to others their rights of conscience, he could not compromise with his own conscience for the sake of any of the flattering advantages offered to the gratifying of a lofty ambition. This persistence in identifying himself with the weaker Non-Conformist party offended those who desired to avail themse ves of his great talents and learning, and who felt that they had as it were a preëmptive right to all distinguished personages in the Realm. For this offense he suffered much annoyance and petty persecutions at their hands. But the Non-Conformist party, grateful for his labors in their cause and for the strength of his name, rallied around him as a leader, and gave him the enthusiasm of their admiration.

At length, being apprehensive of a still further invasion of the rights of conscience, he resolved to migrate to New England, where he could, untrammeled, exercise the Gospel Ministry in accordance with his own sense of duty. This resolution was not made without a struggle, for he ardently loved his native land, was strongly attached to his numerous friends there, and having inherited from his father large real estate, his departure from England would involve much pecuniary loss. But, in spite of all that opposed, his resolution was made, and, with the clearest conviction that he was following the guiding hand of Providence, he sailed with his family and landed in Boston in the summer of the year 1686.

Of his reception in this country and his happy settlement in Bristol, an account has already been given.

On the accession of William to the throne of England, a change was inaugurated which promised greater tolerance and freedom to Dissenters. The heart of Mr. Lee yearned for his native land and the friends of former days, there to enjoy what a few years before had been denied him. Accordingly, to the regret of all who knew him, not only here but throughout New England, he decided to return. After an affectionate parting from his flock in Bristol, he embarked with his family on board the "Dolphin" at Boston. After a boisterous voyage, nearing the coast of Ireland they fell in with a French Privateer, were captured and carried prisoners into the port of St. Maloes, in France. After some detention, his family were allowed to proceed to London, but he was still held as a prisoner. Depression of spirits, solitude and the rigors of winter induced the prison fever which soon terminated his valuable life in December, 1691, aged sixty-four years. Being denounced as a heretic, his body was interred without the walls of the city.*

Mysterious are the ways of Providence. Many of the Lord's chosen are called from the earth in the way of suffering Martyrdom; his Church are left to mourn the loss of these precious ones of their number. But, doubtless, heaven opens to these saints, with joys all the brighter because of their earthly tribulations, and in the triumphs of their faith, those left behind learn important lessons of trust in the darkest hours, and are animated to press forward in the march to final victory.

The Ministry of Mr. Lee in Bristol was very brief, though remarkably fruitful in good results. The Church received additions constantly, and there had been enrolled in its fellowship forty-eight persons. They continued harmonious in all their church relations, and were spiritually profited by the minis-

---

*Sprague's Annals. Allen's Biog. Dict. Dr. Shepard's Hist. Disc. etc.

try of their beloved pastor. His was a Catholic spirit. His learning was united with charity and the poor were often relieved by his bounty. His toils, says tradition, out of the pulpit in visiting the sick and afflicted and administering the consolations of the Gospel, were continuous and faithful; and his preaching was sound, able and eloquent. The following passage from one of his sermons, preserved in the recollection of one of his, people, has been handed down to the present day:

> "Every breath we draw should go forth warm with anthens; the blood's circulation should run around in songs, and every pulse beat upon the strings of David's harp. The wholesome herb should cure our murmurs, and all the creatures of earth, air and water, should by us render a tribute of praise to God."

Mr. Lee kept up an acquaintance with other pastors, and by frequent interchange of views, strengthened them in their work and was himself strengthened in his work. The following extracts from published letters, show how fraternal and cordial was this ministerial intercourse.*

The Rev. Joshua Moody, then associate pastor of the first Church in Boston, in a letter to Increase Mather, then on a visit to England, in 1688, says:

> "Mr. Lee is in Town (tho' going out to-morrow,) Wee spent the 2d instant in your study & had his compy part of the day with us where wee had (blessed be God) a good

---

*Mass. Hist. Coll., VIII., 4th series, 355, 540, 542.

day of Prayer for you and hope in God's good time to have in the same place a day of Praise with you."

The following extracts from letters of Mr. Lee to Mr. Mather, show not only cordial friendship but his interest for the spiritual welfare of the whole region round about as well as for his own parish:

"Aug. 25, '87 Mount Hope.

Deare Mr. Mather. * * * I am compassed with various humors in neighboring towns & Islands, but blissed be God the fogs fly. I have had a long disceptation I cant call a disputation with a stout Anabaptist. But blessed be his holy name they give ground. I am invited to the Island & hope next week to see it, with the Lord's leave & try what work may enter. I want strength of body. I am in a Frontire. You had need incourage us with amunition & auxiliaries from Heaven & to begin to think of some learned, holy, discreet man, that might undertake at Newport. But no more at present. My hearty love to your good son, to my ancient loving friend Mr. Allyn & to my Beloved Brethren Mr. Moody & Mr. Willard, intreating your prayers for strength every way, with hearty respects to my deare sister of whose Turkeys I have so often tasted. Yours affectionately in the Lord. S. L."

"8, 14, 87, Mount Hope.

Deare Mr. Mather,—Methinks its very comfortable to see your hand & had I Dove's wings I would soone see your face with divine permission & a supply, which you can more easily have there. My good ffriend Mr. Morton [Rev. Chas. Morton] has been here. I thank him, but he runs up & down here from place to place & suddenly runs back. That truly I am much troubled at. Once he left me among the bears at Cambridge & now among the

all bears in Rhode Island, but all in Love. Yet I

shall hope when *you* come, you will give me some more of your company. Theres no discoursing under a bit of waxe; but meeting at Heaven's gate with the same petitions, through our gracious Redeemer. I found great respect from the Islanders, as Paul speaks, no little kindness in Malta. One desired me to speak for a young scholar or student to live in his house & teach his children; a man of some quality: but I think will give onely dyet at pr'sent. If any good ffriends would help for about 10 lbs. a y. for clothes: we might begin some work there I hope. I have preacht once there to a few with kind resentmt. & I took occasion by the Judges going in there & would fain have p'suaded Mr. Morton; since the P'sident told him he would provide for his place: but his love to his wife & some other things were his Apology I'intend to give him some account in time God willing. My hearty love to your good son & acquaint him he is in debt a letter to me. To your kind wife & to all our Brethren in the Ministry & in the Lord my wife and drs. pr'sent their hearty resp., especially Anne & so does your truly Lov. Br. & Serv't. in the Ld. S. L."

The following to Mr. Mather, on the eve of his departure on a visit to England, is especially affectionate and kind:

"Febr. 15, 8 7-8.

Deare Good Mr. Mather. Your hearty letter I rec'd as heartily & embraced it *utrisq ulnis & in imo sulce pectoris*. I am glad & sorry of your motion to England *nostri haec farrago libelli*. I doe earnestly desire to sit up one night with you. 3 things hinder as yet. A supply of my place which if you or our f'ds would engage Mr. Metcalf or Mr. Parry to come for 2 or 3 sabbaths I should endeavor to come to you toward the end of next month by the will of God. Another is I expect some things from England in

May & that will double my trouble to come then too. Another is the difficulty of travell to me. But if I get a supply by that time with your loving help & some of our ffds when they come up to you, since my house is as farr from being put in equipage now as in Octob. last; onely hopes begin to spring. There be many things uncommittable to a languid seale, which I remitt, if the Lord p'mitt, to enjoymt. I am shutt off into an Angle from your company; but not from a conversation with you above the circle of human affairs. In haste, longing my letter should quickly see you, subscribe deliberately Your psvering ffd & throu. Grace Br., S. L."

He published several works, among which was a dissertation on "The Ancient and Successive State of the Jews, with Scriptural evidences of their future conversion and establishment in their own land." This was in 1679, and was as able and ingenious a work in advocacy of that theory, which is now held by but few, as was ever published. In 1810, more than thirty years afterwards, Dr. Buchanan, in a sermon before "the Jewish Institution," a benevolent society in England, says,—"It is possible before the end of the present year the four gospels will be published and copies sent to the Jews in the east, as the first fruits of the 'Jewish Institution.' It is very remarkable that this should be the very year which was calculated long ago by a learned man, as that in which 'the times of happiness to Israel' should begin. In the year 1677, Mr. Samuel Lee, a scholar of enlarged views, who had studied the prophetical writings with great attention, published a small volume entitled "Israel Redux" or the Restoration of

Israel. He calculates the event from the prophecies of Daniel, and commences the great period of 1260 years from A. D. 476, which brings it to 1736. He then adds:

'After the great conflicts with the papal powers in the west will begin the stirs and commotions about the Jews and Israel in the East. If then to 1739 we add 30 more they reach to 1766; but the times of perplexity are determined by Daniel to last 45 years longer. If then we conjoin those 45 years more to 1766 it produces one thousand eight hundred and eleven—1811—for those times of happiness to Israel.' "

His other published works were "The Joy of Faith," in 1689; a sermon preached before the Court of Bristol, entitled "The great day of Judgment," in 1691. "The triumph of Mercy," much read in New England, an edition of which was printed in 1718; and "Contemplations on Mortality," respecting which Dr. Allen says, "they display great learning and genius:" Besides these, there were other sermons and smaller works, in all some ten or twelve volumes.

He devoted great attention at one period to the study of Astrology, but afterwards testified his disapprobation of it, by burning his collection of books relating to the subject, a hundred volumes.

As a specimen of his style and exuberance of thought, we give the following extract from his "Triumph of Mercy," p. 27 & foll.

"The Rainbow of the Heavens knows not more rare and delightful colours than the rainbow of the Covenant, under which our Saviour hath placed his Throne. The beauty of a picture shines in variety: which sets such a delicious and pleasant lustre upon prospects and landscapes, where hills and dales, woods and plains, rivers and seas, castles and cities, and the carcases of ancient ruins and hanging rocks are curiously drawn by the Pencil of nature. * * * * * *

God seldom delivers in the same methods. There was never the same face of Heaven from the Creation to this day. The aspects, clouds, and weather do always vary, as the shells on the seashore, and the pebble stones none exactly alike. We have new songs for every moment had we hearts to tune them. When God's wisdom takes one mercy away, his beneficent bounty sends another. When some setting stars dip their flaming rays in the Western Ocean, new ones glitter in the east. Never did the same water bubble from the same fountain: but as God is the inexhaustible spring of new and amiable mercies: So we find he adorns the out-rooms of the world, and the chambers of the Tabernacle of his Church with the Tapestry-hangings of the curious needle-work of his Providence. Such Wisdom dwells with Prudence and finds out the knowledge of witty inventions. All the curiosities of Art and the cunning devices of Artificers are from God: the swarthy Plowman derives his seasons and management of his lands, tillage and culture from Heaven: the women that sit at the wheel, turn it about by the direction of God for the ornaments of the Tabernacle: The weaver, the embroiderer and the ingenious lapidary learnt all in the school which is above the stars; the most admirable of all inventions have dropt into the fancy from the Celestial intelligence. For what the vain unthinking world calls casualty is a graft upon the minds of men cut from the trees of Paradise. * * * * *

And shall we not think that infinite wisdom cannot always present new and ravishing wonders of mercies upon the stage from him who is unconceivable in Counsel and as admirable in working? When we study in this Library we still find new lines and new editions; we sail upon new coasts and see new stars as in the Southern hemisphere, and enjoy a new set of Creatures, and smell at many leagues distant fragrant odoriferous scents; as of Cinnamon from the mountains of Ceylon in India; of Rosemary from Spain; Cedar from Lebanon, that perfume the very thoughts of a Saint; and the further we travel, the more delicious are the surging tops of the hills of Canaan! And the more we taste the more surprising sweetness astonishes our Palates; like the Queen pine in Barbadoes that supplies and transcends expectations with new and rasive favours and tunes our vocal instruments for new songs to bear a part with the Harmony of Angels forever,"

From "The Joy of Faith," p. 6 and foll. we give the following extract, a portion of an argument for the worth of the Scriptures deduced from their "imperial power and efficacy on the souls and consciences of men:"

"Let the world rage in storms of contradiction and like him in Laertius affirm snow to be black, or assert the sun shines not when I see it, or a cordial comforts not when I feel it or that a troubled conscience is but a melancholy fancy, when the terrors of the Lord drink up the spirits of men. These should be sent to Anticyra to purge with Hellebor for madness. Pray, what energy or power can be in a printed paper, in the reading of a chapter wherewith Austin and Iunius were converted from sin to God, or what powerful charm in hearing a mean Preacher, perhaps none of the Learnedest, like the blessed Fishermen of Galilee, to change the heart: if so many proud, haughty and rebellious sinners who of direful persecutors have sometimes turned tender cherishers and protectors of the Church of God: were it not for the fire of the Word of the Lord hosts that melts the stone of the heart and the hammer of that Word that breaks the sturdy Zauzummins all to powder; insomuch that bitter scoffers have been changed into witty Tertullians and turned their satires into panegyricks. What can that be imagined to be that works so strange effects upon whole Nations from the East to the Western-Indies, whitened the Blackmoors, civilized the hearts of Scythians more ragged and brutish than the Rocks and Hyrcanian Tygers that gave them suck and beautified the barbarously painted Britians far beyond the oratory of the Gaules. It could be no other power than the awful dread of the Divine Majesty and the melting sweetness of his Mercy concomitant with his heavenly Word. Wherefore such are justly to be suspected for strangers to the work of grace like Nicodemus at first, tho' a great Doctor in Israel, yet a great dunce in the excellent point of the New-Birth: or like that Doctor at Oxford, sometime since, that searcht the dictionary for the word, and could not tell what to make of it because he found it not there. I say we may greatly fear that they never felt this mighty power of the Spirit of God to change their hearts that dare talk so proudly and irreverently against the self-evidencing power of the holy scriptures on the consciences of men: when the Majesty of God shines ten thousand times brighter in the meridian of that book, than the sun without clouds at noonday in the zenith of Africa."

His sermon, entitled "A summons or warning to the Great Day of Judgment," preached "at the Assizes at Bristol, in N. E., October 7, 1687," was a pictorial scene of soul-moving terror such as few could hear without most serious thought. The text was from Revelation 20: 12: *And I saw the Dead, small and great, stand before God: and the Books were opened: and another Book was opened which is the Book of Life: and the Dead were judged out of those things which were written in the Books, according to their works.* The sermon closed with the following words of exhortation.

1. "As to you the Worthy and Reverend *Judges* that are to sit in judgement before the Lord this day: I shall not enlarge but only present unto you what King Jehoshaphat gave in charge to them from God, when he set them about this work, City by City. *Take heed what you do, for ye judge not for man but the Lord who is with you in the judgment. Wherefore now let the fear of the Lord be upon you. Take heed and do it: for there is no iniquity with the Lord our God, nor respect of Persons, nor taking of gifts.*

2. "To you that are the People and auditors this day Count it a great mercy, that you have been preserved by Restraining or Sanctifying grace, not to stand in the place of the nocent and so to become obnoxious to the wholesom laws & Righteous judgment of the Magistrate. Bless God for that singular mercy: If it were not for the Magistracy, that great ordinance of God in the world, mens tongues would be like poisoned arrows shot forth, speaking deceit, treating their neighbor with their mouths peaceably, and laying wait in their hearts: Some such sons of Belial there are that a man cannot speak to them, they are so surly and interrupting & ought to be thurst away like thorns: if a man touch them he must be fenced with iron & the staff of a spear. Men would prove wolves and vipers; tigers and dragons mixt in one and the same person to each other. O bless God for this great gift of Princes and Judges to rule the wicked and enormous world and to sway the scepter of righteousness in the earth. O Remem-

ber to speak honorably of Rulers and dignities; for they are Ordained of God for the praise of them that do well; and God's Ministers and Avengers upon them that do evil. Were it not for them such as are now but secret, malacious backbiters would soon prove badgers and bite through the bone to the very heart. Have then a special care of two originating sins that lead to many foul enormities, that is pride and envy: First in yourselves that you be not tempted thereby to hurt others: and Secondly in others that you do not hurt them. For wherever you see manifest signatures and tokens of these sins, lurking or putting out their forked tongues against others; beware of them, they are persons marked of God. And always have engraven upon your breast that famous emblem of a righteous man. Do as you would be done by: Tis our Lord's most Golden Rule of Equity: Then judge yourselves before God as to all infirmities, and otherwise insuperable weakness: then fear not man's day: having presented yourselves by Faith as clothed with the Righteousness of Christ and in some sweet measure prepared for that solemn appearance at His Tribunal.

3. "A word or two also to the poor guilty person which has murdered her own unlawful infant, and so I conclude. As for thee poor Creature. What was it that inticed, intangled, inflamed thee to the commission of these sins against the laws of God, the light of nature and the just laws of the land. I understand thus much from thee in the prison; that thy parents were very negligent of thy education, and so becamest a great neglecter of Sabbaths and sermons, and then fellest into the fellowship of lewd companions, which may be a just warning to all others. All that I shall say at present: because of the great Sorrow, remorse & Repentance which thou hast manifested before many witnesses, and I hope may prove sincere: If thou fleest from the horror, stain and shame of these thy crying sins unto the most precious blood in Jesus Christ;

and layest hold upon it with a true though but a weak faith: thou hast patterns of mercy in the blessed book of God: Manassah, Mary Magdalen, and the Thief upon the Cross to dispell their black and dismal cloud of despair: and to lead and incourage thee to hope in His Mercy. To which I humbly and heartily commend thee in the Lord Jesus Christ, the Lord both of Dead and Living. Amen."

Mr. Lee was regarded as one of the most learned and pious men of his day, and was called "the light of both Englands" and "the head and glory of the Church of Bristol." Cotton Mather said of him that "if learning ever merited a statue, this great man has as rich an one due him as can be erected; for it must be granted that hardly ever a more universally learned person trod the American Strand."

### THE MINISTRY LANDS.

The Proprietors of Bristol, among other gifts for the benefit of the town, gave certain tracts of land "for the encouragement and use of an able Gospel Ministry, which land shall remain forever and be for the use of the Ministry for the time being," viz.: One lot on the corner of High and Bradford streets containing two acres, the site of our present Chapel and Church edifices; one twelve acre lot west of "the Commonage;" and one one hundred and fiftieth part of "the Commonage." These lands were designated as "the Ministry Lands."

To these lands others were subsequently added, the gift of individual citizens, viz.: A twelfth part of sixteen and one-half acres, then improved by Madame Dorothy Paine, after her decease, by Will of Charles Church, Esq., dated 1746, November 29th; A lot on the Neck containing ten acres, by Will of Samuel Viall, Esq., dated 1756, May 3d; A lot on the Neck containing about five acres, by Will of Joseph Reynolds, Esq., dated 1757, February 16th.

In the original gift by the Proprietors, the Denomination for whose benefit lands were given was not designated, as only one Church was then contemplated, and it was obviously intended that these lands should be for the benefit of this Church.* But the donors of the additional lands were careful to state that they were "for and towards the support of the Gospel Ministry in the Presbyterian or Congregational way and for no other use or purpose whatsoever."

The lands thus generously given by the founders and early members of the Church have aided very materially in the support of the Gospel Ministry. They are for the most part leased for periods of various lengths of time, and the rents appropriated in accordance with the will of the donors.

---

*Respecting the intention of the donors of the original Ministry lands, we have written evidence of decisive character. On the 30th of March, 1724, Nathaniel Byfield, one of the four Proprietors, gave to Nathaniel Cotton, then pastor of this Church, about six and a half acres of land. In the deed conveying this gift, Mr. Byfield refers to the original deed of Ministry lands, and says, they were "intended to be for the Ministry of the holy Gospel as practiced generally in the Churches of Christ in New England, *which I understand to be Presbyterian and Congregational, which was the design of the four first proprietors of the lands of Mount Hope.*"

# II.

## THE BUILDING GOING FORWARD.–1691-1718.

### EFFORTS TO OBTAIN A PASTOR.

After the departure of Mr. Lee, measures were promptly taken to obtain a successor in the Pastoral Office. Consultation with the Elders in Boston led to the introduction of MR. LEVERETT, of Harvard College, as a candidate for settlement, and on the twenty-ninth of July, 1691, with hearty unanimity, a call was voted. He declined, "because his obligations to the College would not admit of a present acceptance." The call was renewed, with the promise of waiting until the Spring or Summer, "earnestly desiring that he would continue to supply the pulpit meanwhile." He continued to supply until August following, when, on being pressed for a definite answer to the call, he gave a negative reply, and negotiations with him ceased.

After this the Pulpit was supplied by various Ministers in succession, fifteen shillings weekly being paid for the service until 1693, July 24th, when a call was voted to the REV. JOHN SPARHAWK, with a yearly salary of sixty pounds; "five pounds a year additional for firewood, and, after he has a family, ten pounds a year for firewood and the improvement of the Ministry lands." The call was accepted, and he began his labors October 6th following. He continued on trial a year when the following vote was adopted by the town:

"We, the Inhabitants of the Town of Bristol, being met together this 19th day of September, 1694, do, for the maintaining of the Public Worship of God amongst us, and for the Love and Honour we bear to the Rev'd John Sparhawk, and hopes of speedy settlement by him, and for the putting a full and final stop to any further discourse relating to the Strangers' Contribution as an overplus to the Minister (here with us,) do agree upon the considerations abovesaid, and do hereby promise to pay to the said Mr. Sparhawk, by weekly contribution or otherways, within the year the sum of 70 pounds per annum whilst he remains a single man, and 80 pounds for the year when he comes to keep a family, and this we promise during his continuance in the work of the Ministry with us."

With cordial unanimity he was duly installed the second Pastor of the Church, on the twelfth of June, 1695, nearly four years after their sore bereavement in the death of Mr. Lee.

### JOHN SPARHAWK.—SECOND PASTOR.

Mr. Sparhawk was born in 1672, and graduated at Harvard College in 1689, at the youthful age of seventeen years. Respecting his ancestry we have no definite information.

Not long after his settlement in Bristol, he married Priscilla ——, and lived in a house on State street, north of the Common, on or near the spot where now stands the house of P. Hammel, Esq. They had two children, John and Nathaniel, born in 1713 and 1715. The first graduated at Harvard

College in 1733, was ordained at Salem, Mass., 1736, December 8th, and died 1755, April 30th, in the forty-second year of his age.

He died 1718, April 29th, in the twenty-third year of his Ministry, aged forty-six years, and was buried with the tender laments of his people in the cemetery on the Common, near the Sanctuary, where he had faithfully held forth the word of life, being borne to his resting place, from his house, on the shoulders of the office bearers in the Church. His widow survived many years and continued to reside here till her death.

The name of Mr. Sparhawk, as testified by the Rev. Mr. Burt, twenty years after his decease, "remained exceedingly dear and precious to his people." He was a good preacher, and a faithful, judicious pastor. Though not so celebrated as his predecessor, and doubtless a less learned man, he did his work well, and fell at his post his harness on, being called by the Master up higher. The records show that during his Ministry one hundred and two persons were added to the membership of the Church, many others "owned the Covenant," and three hundred and seventy-six children and adults were baptized.

Over his grave his afflicted people erected a memorial stone with the following brief inscription:

"Here Lyeth Interred<br>
ye Body of ye<br>
Reverend MR. JOHN SPARHAWK,<br>
Minister of this Place 23 Years Last Past.<br>
Dyed ye 29th of Aprill, 1718,<br>
in ye 46th year of his age."

## III.

## STORM AND PERIL.—1718-1740.

### THE MCSPARRAN DIFFICULTIES.

After the death of Mr. Sparhawk, there was no settled Pastor for nearly four years. A call was extended to the Rev. Samuel Checkley, who was afterwards the first Pastor of the New South Church in Boston, but he declined it. A call was next voted to James McSparran, a young man who had recently arrived in this country from the north of Ireland as a Licentiate of the Presbytery in Scotland.

"Ye choice of this McSparran," says Mr. Burt, "opened a door to all manner of confusion and disorder. Several scandalous immoralities were soon after reported of him. Dr. Mather, of Boston, and other Ministers, wrote to ye Church by no means to settle him. But ye affections of many towards him for his excellent oratory rendered them slow to believe anything to his disadvantage. Whilst others were as implacably set against him. Two days were set apart for his ordination, but ye Ministers sent for would not lay hands on such a man to separate him to ye work of ye Ministry. But he, being fond of a settlement and hoping to prevail with ye Church, offer'd to submit to a lay ordination. Not long after this it was suspected & yt suspicion was so violent yt, it amounted to little short of proof yt. his credentials from ye Presbytery in Scotland were a counterfeit and a forgery upon wh his opposers were more implacably set against him. October ye 13, 1719, ye Church met at ye motion and desire of Mr.

McSparran to consider whether they ought to give him a Dismission or otherwise permit him to go to Scotland as ye Minister there to clear up his character and to return again. But after considerable debate his dismission was voted ye Church being unwilling to be under a promise of staying for his Return."

It appears from the official records that the Church voted, on the 16th of December, 1718, to call him to the Pastoral office; on the 22d of December following, the town, by a vote of seventy to three, concurred in the Church's choice; on the 19th of April following, arrangements were made to call a Council for his ordination. There is no official record of the doings of Council. On the 25th of May following, the town adopted this minute:

"The accounts lately received from Barnstable and Plymouth in favor of the Rev'd Mr. James McSparran being read in publick Town Meeting together with our own experience of his good conversation during his abode in this Town and his humble Christian deportment under the present afflictive Providence, with his ready acknowledgement of his ungaurded conversation in times past, with his earnest desire under his hand which hath been now read to be reconciled to the Church of Christ, demand our Christian compassion in the exercise of that fervent charity which covers the multitude of sins. We do in duty, as well as affection, declare our hearty forgiveness of all his past miscarriages and that we do receive him as our Brother in the Lord, humbly depending upon the boundless mercy and compassion of our most gracious God through the merits of our blessed Redeemer ye Lord Jesus Christ for pardon and acceptance. We most earnestly desire that all Christian People referring to this our dear and Rev'd Brother, Mr. James McSparran, would put on charity which is the bond of perfectness and all these scandalous Reports that have been spread abroad will, as they ought, be buried in oblivion."

"The above writing being distinctly read in the Town meeting, and people being asked whether they had any objection against it or any part of it, it was unanimously voted in ye affirmative as the mind of ye town, no one objecting after ye vote was called except Conll Paine.

Attest: SAMUEL HOWLAND, Town Clerk."

The way now seemed clear for his settlement in regular order. Accordingly, arrangements were made to call a Council for this purpose on Thursday, October 22d, following. Before this day arrived, the new report of forgery of credentials broke out and threw matters into worse confusion than before. Without waiting for the meeting of Council he proposed to withdraw at once if the Church and town would give him an honorable dismission, or to return to Scotland and obtain confirmation of his credentials, if they would grant him leave of absence. As stated by Mr. Burt, the Church voted his dismission, but the town would not concur in this action but adopted the following vote, viz.:

"Voted, that Leave is given by the Town to Mr. James McSparran, our present Minister, to take a voyage to Ireland, in order to procure a confirmation of his credentials, the truth of which being by some questioned: and that he return to us again sometime in June next ensuing, and proceed in ye work of the Ministry with us if he procure ye confirmation of ye aforesaid credentials."

On the 20th of June, 1720, having heard nothing from Mr. McSparran, the Town voted to extend his leave of absence to the 16th of September following. This period also passed without his return, or any report from him, and the town was then ready to coöperate with the Church in securing another Pastor.

While the town were thus patiently waiting for their Minister's return, he was abroad taking Orders in the Church of England. On the 21st of August, 1720, he was admitted to Deacon's Orders by the Bishop of London. On the 25th of September following, he was ordained to the Priesthood by the Archbishop of Canterbury. On the 23d of October following, he was commissioned by the Bishop of London "to discharge the Ministerial Office in the Province of New England in America." Under the patronage of "the Society for the Propagation of the Gospel in Foreign Parts," he came back commissioned as a "Missionary to Narragansett in New England, who is to officiate as opportunity shall offer at Bristol, Freetown, Swanzey, and Little Compton, where there are many people, members of the Church of England, destitute of a Minister."

### DAY OF PRAYER AND CHOICE OF PASTOR.

On the 22d of September, 1720, the Church set apart the 1st of October following as a day of fasting and prayer, in view of the present unhappy condition of affairs. To assist in the services of the day they invited the Rev. Messrs. Thatcher, of Milton; Danforth, of Freetown; Wadsworth, of Boston; White, of Attleborough; Fisher, of Dighton; Billings, of Little Compton; and Clapp, of Newport. The day was one of great spiritual profit, and a fitting preparation for choosing and settling a Pastor, which was not long after accomplished.

On the 22d of December, 1720, the Centennial Anniversary of the landing of the Pilgrims at Plymouth, the Church, by nearly an unanimous vote, chose the Rev. Nathaniel Cotton for their Pastor, and on the 23d and 30th of January following, the town "by a very considerable majority of votes," gave its concurrence and proposed, for his encouragement to settle, one hundred pounds; also, one hundred pounds yearly salary beginning with the 1st of January, and the Strangers' Contribution. Subsequently the improvement of the Ministry lands was added. The call was accepted, and on the 31st of August, 1721, he was duly ordained the third in the succession of Pastors of this Ancient Church. The sermon on the occasion was by the Rev. Joseph Belcher, of Dedham.

### NATHANIEL COTTON.—THIRD PASTOR.

Mr. Cotton was a descendant of the distinguished John Cotton who came to Boston from England in 1633, who, being then about forty-eight years of age, of large and varied experience, and eminent for his talents, learning and piety, was soon designated and set apart as Teacher of the First Church, of which the Rev. John Wilson was Pastor, whose labors were attended with such remarkable blessing that during the first five years a greater number were admitted to his Church than to all the other Churches in the Colony, and who died on the 23d of December, 1652, in the sixty-eighth year of his age, lamented as a public loss in all the Churches in the country.

He was a son of the Rev. Roland Cotton, of Sandwich, Mass., born in 1698, graduated at Harvard College in 1717, and was therefore only twenty-three years of age when he assumed the Pastoral Office in Bristol. His father was a grandson of the Rev. John Cotton, above mentioned, and one of several Congregational Ministers whom this family produced, all of whom were eminent for their piety and usefulness. His younger brother, Josiah, graduated at Harvard in 1722, and was ordained Pastor of the Beneficient Church in Providence, 1728, October 23d, which office he held for several years, and was afterwards settled at Woburn, Mass., and Sandown, N. H., and died 1780, May 27, aged seventy-eight years.

Not long after his settlement he married the widow of Mr. William Sanford, of Newport, and lived, it is supposed, in the house on State street, which had been previously occupied by Mr. Sparhawk, and, after his decease, by his widow.

His Ministry was continued under the embarrassments which grew out of the McSparran difficulties until his strength failed, and he sank to an early grave 1729, July 3d, in the thirty-first year of his age. But, though troubled and brief, his Ministry was fruitful in good results. Many were added to the Church on Profession of Faith, others "owned the Covenant," and over a hundred children and adults were baptized. The House of Worship was also thoroughly repaired and improved, and the courage and hope of the church failed not.

The Rev. Mr. Burt says of him, "he was a man of singular prudence, of admirable patience, and for the cause of Truth and Righteousness he was as bold as a lion, and his name continued fresh in the memories and exceeding dear and precious to his people." He made his grave with his beloved flock, and a Memorial stone was erected with the following inscription:

Here lies the remains of

THE REV. MR. NATHANIEL COTTON, M. A.,

and Pastor of ye Church in this Town.

Born at Sandwich, June ye 16, 1698,

2d son of ye late REV. MR. ROLAND COTTON,

and his wife ELIZ., only daughter of ye HON.

NATHANIEL SALLONSTALL, ESQ., of Haverhill.

Took his degrees at H. College 1717 and 1720.

Ordained here Aug. 30, 1721.

Married ye relect of MR. WILLIAM SANFORD, of Newport,

By whom he had 4 sons and 4 daughters.

Died here July 3d, 1729,

Greatly Valued and Lamented.

## BARNABAS TAYLOR.—FOURTH PASTOR.

Shortly after the decease of Mr. Cotton, the Church and Town, with a remarkable degree of unanimity, united in calling the REV. BARNABAS TAYLOR, voting him two hundred pounds for settlement, and a yearly salary of one hundred and forty pounds, together with the use or income of the Ministry lands and the Strangers' Contribution. The call was accepted and he was duly installed the fourth Pastor, 1729, December 25th.

There are no Church records during his Ministry and we have no means of knowing any fruits of his labors. Mr. Burt says, "he was much admired at first;" but for some cause respecting which the record is silent he failed to give satisfaction, and, by the advice of an Ecclesiastical Council, was dismissed 1740, June 3d.

# IV.

## PEACE AND PROSPERITY.—1740–1775.

### JOHN BURT.—FIFTH PASTOR.

Very soon after the dismission of Mr. Taylor, the Rev. John Burt was introduced to the Church, and began to preach in July, 1740, as a candidate for settlement. On the 17th of November following, he was unanimously chosen to the Pastoral office. On the 5th of January, 1741, the Town voted unanimously to concur in the Church's choice, and for his support proposed a yearly salary of two hundred and fifty pounds in silver money, at twenty-eight shillings per ounce or its equivalent in paper currency, the Strangers' Contribution, and the improvement of the Parsonage house and Ministry lands. The call was accepted, and on the 13th of May, 1741, he was duly ordained and installed the fifth Pastor by a Council consisting of the Elders and Messengers of Churches in Boston, Newport, Little Compton, Dighton, Rehoboth, Attleborough and Providence. The sermon on the occasion was preached by himself, from 2d Cor. v. 20. The charge to the Pastor was given by the Rev. Mr. Webb, of Boston, who was the Pastor of his childhood and the Instructor of his riper years. The right hand of fellowship was given by the Rev. Mr. Turner, of Rehoboth. And the prayer was offered by the Rev. Mr. Fisher, of Dighton, the Moderator of the Council.

MR. BURT was a native of Boston; born 1716, graduated at Harvard College, 1736, at twenty years of age. After graduation he pursued his studies for the Ministry under the direction of his Pastor. He remained in the Pastorate to the day of his death, 1775, October 7th, in the thirty-fifth year of his Ministry and the fifty-ninth year of his age.

His house was on Hope street, near the present mansion of Mrs. Scott Greene. During the attack of the British on the town, 1777, May 25th, this was the first house which was fired and destroyed.

On taking charge of the Church he gathered what information he could respecting its history and present condition, and prefaced an account to a book of records which he faithfully kept during his entire ministry, and for neatness of copy and fullness they are much in advance of any kept by his predecessors. At the beginning of his Ministry seventy-seven names appear on his record as being at that time members in full communion. Additions were continually made, and, at his death, sixty-five members had been received to full communion, one hundred and eighteen others had "owned Covenant," and five hundred and twenty-six children and adults had been baptized.

His Ministry was eminently successful. A faithful, bold and earnest preacher, and a judicious counsellor and friend, he won the respect of all classes, and enjoyed, in a marked degree, the confidence and affection of his people. This period was emphatically one of peace and prosperity. The bitterness of the McSparran controversey had greatly abated; measures for the support of the Gospel were adopted which were generally satisfactory, and a steady devotion to the cause of Christ produced its fruits of joy and harmony.

In 1746, by Commissioners, the Town of Bristol, with four other towns, was set off from Massachusetts and annexed to Rhode Island. As by the fundamental law of this State, the support of religious institutions could only be by voluntary contribution, the Church could no longer look to the town for support as formerly, but must rely upon its own special friends and helpers. But, previous to this, an arrangement was made with the town, whereby those who chose to have their Ministry taxes go towards the support of the Ministry of another order could do so by properly signifying their wish to the town authorities.

On the 7th of October, 1775, there passed away from earth this Pastor beloved. Tenderly was his body laid away to rest in the cemetery on the Common, where sleep the mortal remains of Sparhawk and Cotton, and as a tribute to his memory a tablet with the following inscription was erected by his mourning people:

Sacred to the Memory
of the REV. JOHN BURT, A. M.,
born in Boston, educated at Harvard University;
Ordained pastor of the Congregational Church
in Bristol, May 13, A. D. 1741.
He died aged 59 on the 7th of Oct. 1775,
in the evening of the ever memorable
Bombardment of this Town
by a British Squadron.
*He was the noble advocate*
*of Civil Liberty and religious Freedom,*
*and a faithful Pastor to his Flock.*
His Parishioners
from a sincere respect
for his many virtues,
and a just veneration
of his excellent character
have erected this Monument
to his MEMORY.

# V.

## HALTING OF THE WORK.—1775-1785.

### THE FLOCK SCATTERED WITHOUT A SHEPHERD.

In 1775, Bristol was a flourishing commercial town with a population which numbered about twelve hundred and fifty. On the breaking out of the Revolutionary war, the town took prompt measures to perform its part in the memorable conflict, and its history during this period is one of thrilling interest. "Some time during the summer, a British squadron arrived in Newport, and lay there until the 7th of October, on the morning of which day an express arrived here with the news that the squadron was getting under weigh at Newport, with the intention of sailing to Bristol. This news caused much alarm and confusion throughout the town. The day of the occurrence was unusually pleasant. About three o'clock in the afternoon, the squadron, consisting of three ships of war, named the Rose, the Gaspee, and the Eskew, with a bomb brig and a schooner, was seen standing up the bay in full sail, with a gentle breeze to the south. Shortly after sunset they were anchored in our harbor, making a display such as never was seen here before or since. Wallace, in the Rose, took the lead, run up and anchored within a cable's length of Market wharf. The Gaspee next came up and anchored about a cable's length to the south. The other attempting to go farther south grounded on the middle ground. The schooner ran up and anchored opposite the bridge. At eight o'clock a royal salute was fired from the flag ship. Shortly after the salute a barge left the flag ship, and was pulled in to the wharf where a large number of the citizens were congregated. The commanding officer having stepped upon the wharf, communicated the fact that Captain James Wallace, commander of the squadron, had sent him with a demand for forty sheep and a pair of oxen; and if they were refused he should fire upon the town. The Town Council were immediately called together, and the demand of the British was laid before them. After some discussion upon the subject the Council decided that the demand was unreasonable, and that they would not comply with it. 'Is this your final answer?' asked the commander. 'Yes, yes,' shouted many unfaltering voices in reply. The officer immediately jumped into the barge and pulled towards the ship. In a short time after the barge returned, the report of a cannon, fired from the flag ship, was heard. The other ships then commenced firing upon the town, and the flashes of the cannon, the whistling of the balls through the air, the bursting of bombs, was a scene terrible in the extreme. The bomb brig threw carcasses (machines made of iron hoops and filled with all manner of combustibles) to set fire to the town. They were thrown up nearly perpendicular, with a tremendous tail to them, and when they fell to the ground they blazed up several yards high."

"Horror and dismay were depicted on every countenance, women and children crying and screaming were seen running through the streets in every direction to seek some place of safety. Many of them were removed to the farms and remote parts of the town while the balls were whistling over their heads as they went. The firing continued for about an hour when a citizen standing upon a point of land which made off some distance in the harbor, succeeded in hailing the commander of the squadron, and the firing was suspended. An epidemic was raging in town, which had proved fatal in many cases, and at this time three persons lay dead in their dwellings, while the remains of Governor Bradford's wife had been buried but the day before. Letters were sent on board stating these facts and promising to comply with the demand if they would stop firing. One account says: 'While preparations were being made to send the sheep on board, Captain Martin, of Seekonk, arrived with a company of men and protested they should not be sent. Bringing his field pieces upon a small eminence that commanded the bay, he commenced firing upon the enemy's shipping. Opposed thus unexpectedly and placed now at a disadvantage to renew the contest, the ships of Wallace made their way back to Newport.' But from the town records it appears that the town paid for sheep furnished by citizens and delivered to Captain Wallace; and an account written by an eye witness says, 'In the morning we returned to our dwellings, and on coming up Main street we saw the British squadron standing out of the harbor bound to Newport.' If Wallace was defeated and driven out by Martin, it could not have been until the next morning."

"It is wonderful that there was no person killed. There were many hair breadth escapes from death. A little lad three and one-half years old, accompanying his mother in flight, a cannon ball struck the limb of a tree on their left hand which, severed from the trunk, fell directly at their side. As Governor Bradford, who in the name of the town refused compliance with the demand for sheep and cattle, was returning to his house through his garden, as he was climbing the fence, the board on which his hand rested was knocked from his grasp by a cannon ball. A man went to a well to get water to put out one of the "carcasses" which fell near his house, and he had scarcely left the well when a cannon ball struck the curb which was shattered to pieces."

"The only person who died during this attack was the REV. JOHN BURT, who was afterwards found dead lying on his face on a hill of corn. A nine pound shot was dug from the earth at a short distance from him, and in an exact range of him and the ship, but no marks of its effects were found upon his body. An inquest was held before Daniel Bradford, Esq., coroner, and the verdict of the Jury was, that 'he, being for sometime past sick and languid, was surprised by a cannonading upon the town of Bristol, on the evening before his heath, abdicated his house, attended by nobody, either got lost and bewildered, or was seized by some sudden fit and so came to his death.'"

The day following was Sunday, and a day of solemn sadness to the people who gathered in the Sanctuary and learned that the voice of their beloved Pastor was hushed in death. A great gloom settled over the community, and many hearts bowed to God in tearful prayer.

The thoughts of the people were now chiefly given up to the war. But the few families who were not driven abroad made great efforts to keep the pulpit supplied during most of this gloomy period. The following ministers officiated, viz.: the REV. MESSRS. AMASA LEONARD, GEORGE MOREY, HUNTINGDON PORTER, JOSEPH DAVIS, ALLEN OLCOTT, ELIPHALIT PORTER, THOMAS ROBY, SAMUEL SHUTTLESWORTH, HENRY CHANNING, ASA PIPER, and JUDE DAMON.

On the 25th of May, 1777, the town received the severest blow of the war. In the morning "about five hundred British and Hessian troops, under the command of Lieutenant Colonel Campbell, started from Newport in a ship of war. Before daylight they anchored about half a mile south of Peck's rocks, on the west side of Pappoosquaw. They immediately landed and marched through Warren to the Kickamuit river. A number of boats belonging to the State had been collected here. The British heaped these boats together and burnt them. They then marched back to Warren where they took a number of prisoners and burned the Baptist Church, a powder magazine, and a number of dwelling houses. They delayed here but a short time, as they feared an attack from the American militia. They then marched down the main road to Bristol, plundering houses and taking the men prisoners. The inhabitants of Bristol were filled with consternation, as on account of the special enmity of the British to this town they had every reason to expect the most severe treatment. At this time a regiment of militia, commanded by Colonel Cary, and a company of artillery, Captain Pearce, were stationed in the town. The militia were quartered in different dwelling houses on Hope street, and the artillery in a house on the corner of Hope and Burton streets. Word was brought to the commander of the troops that a large force of British were coming down the main road. Their numbers were probably much exaggerated. As he had but about three hundred and fifty men he deemed it advisable not to engage with the British, and accordingly marched his men out of town to the back road. The artillery company marched up Burton street to Wood street and there halted."

"Meanwhile the British entered the town. They continued to make all the men prisoners, but refrained from injuring the houses until they reached the large dwelling house where the Rev. Mr. Burt had lived, which they burnt to the ground. The work of destruction thus commenced soon became general. The houses in which the troops had been quartered were all burnt. On the east side of Hope street all the houses were burnt, from Mr. Burts' to Byfield street except the Oxx house. On the west side all to the Episcopal Church, which was also burnt. The square below the Church was then a meadow, unoccupied with buildings. Eighteen dwellings and a number of other buildings were destroyed, and between thirty and forty men were taken prisoners."

"As soon as the British landed, an express was sent to General Sullivan in Providence, intelligence reaching him about eight o'clock in the morning. By his direction, Colonel Barton, with a few horsemen, started for Bristol. The regiment which had marched to the back road returned down Mount lane, and passing down High street marched in pursuit of the British who were then crossing Walker's bridge. As soon as the enemy made their appearance the artillery commenced firing upon them, and pursued them to the Ferry, firing all the time. By the blood in the road it was supposed that a considerable number of the British were killed or wounded. A large number of militia now poured into the town, but they were too late to be of any service. The ship which brought the British from Newport, after having sent a boat on shore and taken captive Captain Westcott and nine American privates who were on Pappoosquaw got under weigh, and sailed to the Ferry for the purpose of taking off the British, which was successfully accomplished."

"This attack of the British left the town in a wretched condition. Nearly every house on the principal street was reduced to ashes. It is probable that if the British had not been closely pursued they would have burnt the entire town. In addition to the loss of their houses, the inhabitants were obliged to endure poverty and want, as provisions were scarce and prices consequently high. A large number of soldiers were constantly quartered among them, and they were obliged to submit to all the inconveniences of a garrisoned town. They were kept in a state of continued alarm, and their slumbers were broken nearly every night. The fences were all torn down for fuel, and the land for nearly two miles out of town laid waste. Many of the in habitants left their homes taking their personal effects with them."

Under these trying circumstances, continued through the period of the war, it could hardly be otherwise that Zion should languish, and the work of building her walls halt and almost cease. But though cast down she was not destroyed. Her life, though feeble, still breathed, and in due time a brighter day dawned.

The foregoing account is chiefly condensed from "Annals of Bristol," a series of papers published in "The Bristol Phenix," in 1845.

## VI.

## THE WORK RESUMED.—1785-1812.

### THE CATHOLIC SOCIETY ORGANIZED.

At the close of the war, as soon as the town began to rally from its long prostration, the friends of the Congregational Church took measures to resume with new vigor the work of building up Zion. Some of the leading members of the Congregation at a meeting, 1783, March 31st, opened a scheme for a fund, "the annual interest of which to be appropriated for the support of an Orthodox Congregational Minister." At a meeting, 1784, September 6th, it was voted to petition the General Assembly for an Act of Incorporation.

The Charter of the "Catholic Congregational Society, of Bristol, R. I.," was granted by the General Assembly of the State, 1784, October 4th, "for the purpose of raising a fund by free and voluntary subscriptions, contributions, legacies and donations, for the support of public worship in the Congregational Society in the town of Bristol, of which the Rev. John Burt was the late Pastor."

By the terms of the Charter the Society were restricted to the raising of moneys for the purposes named only, "by free and voluntary subscription, contribution, legacy or donation." And if ever there shall be a less number than nine members, then

" all moneys, bonds, mortgages, deeds, notes, obligations, books and papers of every kind, together with all the estate, both real and personal, whatsoever at that time belonging to the said Catholic Society, shall be given up to and the sole property thereof be vested in the Congregational Society aforesaid, for whose use and benefit the said Catholic Society is instituted."

This Society have continued to act in coöperation with the Church to the present day. The " Ministry Lands," originally entrusted to the town, naturally and properly fell to the care of the Catholic Society, and all the arrangements for the support of the Gospel Ministry and for meeting the current expenses of the Church are under its direction.

### ERECTION OF THE SECOND HOUSE OF WORSHIP.

Soon after the organization of the Catholic Society, measures were taken for the erection of a new house of worship. The site chosen was at the corner of Hope and Bradford streets. The house was raised, 1784, June 12th, and was finished and dedicated to Almighty God, 1785, January 5th, the day of the ordination of the Rev. Henry Wight. The house was of the style of architecture common at that period, with square pews, high pulpit, Deacon's seat in front, and sounding board overhead. At a later period it was thoroughly renovated in the interior by substituting for the square pews the modern style of slips, and neatly covering the walls with " hard finish." It served the congregation until the erection of the present house in 1856, when it was given to the town, who removed it to its present site, on the north side of Bradford street, and having thoroughly remodeled the interior, with but little change in the exterior, have since used it for Town purposes.

### HENRY WIGHT, D. D.—SIXTH PASTOR.

The Rev. Henry Wight, born in Medfield, Mass., in 1753, graduated at Harvard College in 1782, began to preach here 1784, March 14th, and being unanimously chosen to the Pastoral office with the hearty concurrence of the newly formed Catholic Society, he was ordained 1785, January 5th, in connection with the interesting services of dedicating the new house of worship. The sermon on this occasion was by the Rev. Thomas Prentiss, Pastor of the Church in Medfield, Mass., in which Mr. Wight was baptized in infancy and had passed his early years, from the text 2 Corinthians, vi. 3, 4. The ordaining prayer and charge to the Pastor were by the Rev. Solomon Townsend, of Barrington, and the Right-hand of Fellowship by the Rev. Robert Rogerson, of Rehoboth, Mass.

Very soon after the installation of Mr. Wight, the list of Church members was revised, and was found to contain thirty-six names of persons then living, of whom seven were males and twenty-nine were females. On the 21st of March, 1785, the custom of "owning Covenant" which had previously prevailed was abolished by the following votes:

"Voted, that the half-way Covenant is not consistent with the spirit of the Gospel, and a hindrance to vital piety.

"Voted, that hereafter this Church will have but one Covenant for admission of members to their body."

Dr. Wight continued in the sole pastorate of the Church until 1815, November 13th, when the REV. JOEL MANN was ordained as Colleague Pastor. On the 11th of November, 1828, at his own request, he was dismissed by an Ecclesiastical Council, but continued to reside among his people to the day of his death, in August, 1837, in the eighty-sixth year of his age. His residence was at the corner of High and Bradford streets, the house now occupied by William H. Spooner, Esq. His family consisted of several sons and daughters, who grew up in the Christian faith, and adorned the stations of life which they were called to fill. The eldest, JOHN B. WIGHT, was ordained Pastor of the Congregational Church in East Sudbury, Mass., 1815, January 25th. The sermon on the occasion, which was published with the other parts of the services by the Church, was from Matthew xxviii. 20, by the REV. JOSEPH MCKEAN, LL. D., Professor in Harvard College. The Charge to the Pastor was by his father.

From 1793 to 1833, Dr. Wight was a member of the Board of Fellows of Brown University, and in 1811 received from thence the degree of Doctor in Divinity.

His ministry, continuing for nearly half a century, longer than that of any other pastor, was characterized by Catholicity in intercourse with other denominations, and an amiability of spirit and fidelity to his convictions of right, which won respect and confidence. He took an active interest in the political questions of the day, and did not hesitate to introduce topics of this nature in his pulpit ministrations, which offended some whose views differed from his and led to their withdrawal from the Society. He was singularly faithful in recording all the votes of the Church, and even the informal proceedings of Conferences and Committee meetings. He also kept for many years quite a full record of current events in the town, particularly of marriages and deaths, and this book has already proved to be of invaluable worth in proving titles to property and to the bounties and pay of soldiers and others who died in the Governmental service.

During the sole pastorate of Dr. Wight, there were two hundred and twenty-eight additions to the Church membership, and a large number of children and adults were baptized.

His memory is precious to the aged few who yet survive to recall his labors in the days of his strength. The marks of his influence are indelibly traced in the character of the community; and in the great day of account we doubt not it will be said of this man, "Well done, good and faithful servant, enter thou into the joy of thy Lord."

His mortal remains rest in the Juniper Hill Cemetery, and over his grave is erected a memorial stone with the following inscription:

"The Grave of
REV. HENRY WIGHT, D. D.,
Born in Medfield, Mass.,
May 26, 1752.
Graduated
at Harvard College, 1782:
Settled over the Cong. Church
in this place Jan. 5, 1785.
Deceased Aug. 12, 1837,
in the 86th year
of his age,
and the 53d of his ministry.

—:o:—

Faithful and kind in the duties
of his sacred office,
Affectionate and tender
in the relations of domestic life,
his memory is precious
to his surviving kindred and people.
With long life was he satisfied
and his end was peace.

—:o:—

*Remember the words which I spake unto you
while I was yet present with you.*"

—:o:—

# VII.

## THE PERIOD OF REVIVALS.—1812–1830.

### THE REVIVAL OF 1812.

Revivals of Religion of remarkable depth and power were enjoyed by many of the Churches of New England during the early part of the present century.

The first signal awakening of this description in this town began to be developed in the summer of 1812, and was promoted through the united efforts of all the Churches among whom there prevailed a delightful harmony.

The Rev. Isaac Lewis, D. D., of New York, as he was journeying with his wife for her health, tarried for a night in Bristol. Learning of the interesting state of the public mind on the subject of personal religion, he was induced to remain a few days to participate in the good work. It was arranged that he should preach on a week day in the Congregational house, and notice of the service was circulated as far as practicable. As the hour of meeting approached the people *en masse* turned from their shops, their farms and their homes, and flocked to the Sanctuary. An air of solemnity and earnestness pervaded the crowded assembly. Even those who came from curiosity, or from an impulse which they could hardly define, as they crossed the threshold of the House of God, were deeply impressed with the thought that it was an hour of supreme importance to them. The preacher felt the inspiration of the occasion, and preached from the text "Remember now thy Creator in the days of thy youth," Eccles. xii. 1. The vast audience were deeply moved. Many were convicted of sin and a number then and there resolved to be at peace with God.

From this time the Revival progressed in depth and power, and the labors of DR. LEWIS, in coöperation with the pastors, were greatly blessed. Many were converted. Persons who had grown old in sin, broken hearted turned unto the Lord and received pardon. Men and women encompassed by the cares of this world and eagerly pursuing its riches were arrested to care for their never-dying souls and to obtain the enduring riches of heaven. Young men and maidens in the vigor of their strength laid their all upon the altar of God and entered upon the Christian service. For many months the whole interest of the people was absorbed in this mighty work of the Spirit, and the incidents connected with it remained the subject of delightful and thankful record while any of the generation lived who had been made partakers of it.

The influence of this Revival extended to other towns and Churches, and in many places its impressions were indellible. At one time, a party of young men from west of the Bay came in a boat for the express purpose of having a "rollicking time," and to disturb the meetings. The Spirit of God met them here and some of the number were converted, returned home to carry the good influence with them, and became eminently devoted Christians.

All the Churches in Bristol shared in this glorious Revival. The venerable Dr. Griswold, Rector of St. Michael's Espiscopal Church, was also Bishop of the Diocese which then embraced all the New England States. Entering cordially into the work, his influence was felt not only in his own Church, which, under his Ministry and the holy influence that pervaded the town, glowed with large results of the Divine Blessing, but throughout the Diocese giving new character and life to many of the Churches. Around him as a leader and example gathered the evangelical elements of the body, and from his Ministry and Episcopate, the distinguishing sentiments of the Evangelical party received their organized shape and tone.

Dr. Wight, the pastor of this Church, being advanced in life, from the infirmities of age, could do but little beside the routine work of his calling. Under these circumstances Dr. Lewis was employed as an assistant for a period of six months, and invited to settle as Colleague Pastor. This he declined, but during his temporary engagement instituted a class for Doctrinal instruction, embracing over a hundred persons, chiefly converts of the Revival in our congregation. The class met weekly and recited lessons from the Assembly's Shorter Catechism. These were accompanied by familiar but elaborate lectures on the doctrines of the Bible

*By this means Christians were rooted and grounded in the faith, and an Evangelical tone was given to the Church which has ever since characterized it.*

The fruits of this gracious Revival were remarkably permanent and abiding. The Sabbath services were crowded with attendants. The congregations were serious, earnest, and engaged in worship. The people listened to the faithful preaching of the Gospel with unbroken interest. The meetings for private worship and instruction in the week were well attended. A religious spirit was the very atmosphere of the place, and the people were united, ready and earnest in every good work. This was the immediate fruit and influence of the great revival of 1812. To the few surviving subjects of it, the recollection to this day is most precious. Their countenances are animated with joy, and their lips are tremulous with grateful emotion, as they speak of the gracious scenes of this remarkable awakening sixty years ago.

### JOEL MANN.—SEVENTH PASTOR.

The great revival of 1812 and its results, prepared the way for the settlement of the REV. JOEL MANN, the Seventh Pastor, 1815, November 15th, as a Colleague with DR. WIGHT. He was a native of Oxford, N. H., and graduated at Dartmouth College in 1812. He remained in the Pastoral office until 1826, September 14th, when, at his request, he was dismissed by Ecclesiastical Council, and was afterwards settled in Kingston, Greenwich, Conn., and Salem, Mass.

His Ministry was eminently successful, and was particularly distinguished for the institution of the Sabbath School, the great revival of 1820, and the erection of "the Hall," accounts of which are given further on. He is still living in a remarkably vigorous old age in Brooklyn, N. Y., and is cordially received by his friends and former parishioners on his annual visits to the town.

His residence here was on Bradford street, a few rods east from the present Parsonage, in a house recently owned and occupied by Messadore T. Bennett, Esq., which was destroyed by fire on the 4th of July, 1870.

### THE SABBATH SCHOOL BEGUN.

The Sabbath school was first instituted in the town of Bristol in the spring of 1815. Miss Susan Wyatt, associating with herself three others, viz.: Miss Mary A. Bourne, Miss Abby Monroe, and Miss Waity Sanford, opened a school on Sunday afternoons at five o'clock in the school room of her father, Mr. Stutely Wyatt, on High street. This school continued in successful operation until the approach of winter when it was discontinued.

The following year, 1816, Miss Mary T. Borden (afterwards Mrs. Nathaniel Gladding,) opened a school in the south-west basement room of the house on Hope street, now owned and occupied by James E. French, Esq., where she also kept a day school for many years. Here for several years Miss Borden, assisted by members of the Church, gave Sabbath instruction to the young. From a small beginning the school grew in interest and importance until in 1820, June 26th, the Church, by a formal vote, took the school under its own charge, appointed a committee to conduct its affairs, and chose teachers for the several classes.

From this time to the present the school has been under the fostering care of the Church, and is regarded not as a separate institution but as a field of labor for which the Church is responsible. The Superintendent, nominated by the teachers, is elected by the Church at the annual meeting, and to the Church he makes an annual report of its condition.

Previous to 1865, the school was held successively in private rooms and in the various "Halls" that had been provided for conference meetings, etc. But the growth of the school made it necessary to secure a larger place for its sessions, and in the autumn of that year the school was transferred to the House of Worship and was soon doubled in numbers. Here its sessions were regularly held until the completion of the "Memorial Chapel" in 1870, in whose beautiful and convenient rooms it has at last found a Home.

A library of about six hundred volumes is connected with the school, arranged in three departments, Youths', Intermediate, and Adult, to which additions are annually made.

### THE REVIVAL OF 1820.

During the Winter and Spring of 1819-20, another

season of extraordinary refreshing from on high was enjoyed. Previous to its manifestation there was nothing special to awaken expectations of it, save that in the weekly meetings of conference and prayer and the Sabbath services an earnest evangelical spirit prevailed, the habit of family prayer was generally maintained, and songs of praise were heard in the evening hour from many an habitation. Respecting the progress of this Revival the pastor, the Rev. Joel Mann, writes as follows:

"The meetings became more frequent, and as room in a private house was not sufficient to accommodate the people, they were transferred to the second story of a cabinet-maker's shop. Here was displayed the power and grace of God, from day to day, in a signal manner. It was the place in which many submitted to the Lord, and found joy and peace in believing.

"This room became so filled as to be uncomfortable, and another, over a carriage house, was prepared and seated at considerable expense.

"This proving too strait, meetings were held in the church, and at length the large room in the Court House was obtained, which was occupied and filled from evening to evening for many weeks, until needed for a session of the court. Here cases of conscience were tried and decided. Here the Omniscient Judge presided, and trembling sinners were arraigned and made to feel and acknowledge their guilt. Here long-standing controversies were settled between Him and them. Here violaters of divine law were convicted, owned the justice of their condemnation, submitted to the disposal of the Judge, and obtained pardoning mercy. The pleadings of God's people were heard, and the blessings for which they sued were granted. The voices of converts proclaimed the riches of divine grace, the wonders of redeeming love, and songs of praise burst forth on every side. The Lord Jesus held His court there, presented an indictment to the conscience of many a sinner, made him plead guilty, and then discharged him with full and free forgiveness. The scenes enacted there made a new swell of joy in heaven, and brought glory and praise to the divine head of the Church."

As in the Revival of 1812, so in this the work was shared by all the Churches in town, and a delightful spirit of Catholic union prevailed. Bishop Griswold, the Rector of St. Michael's Church, had, under his charge, several students for the Ministry, among whom was the venerable Stephen H. Tyng, Sr., D. D., of New York city. Being suddenly prostrated by sickness, the responsibility of guiding inquirers, holding conference and prayer meetings, etc., devolved largely upon these students who, under the blessing of the Spirit in this remarkable work, received an impulse and a tone of piety which, in subsequent years, distinguished them as Evangelical preachers and earnest winners of souls. The name of Dr. Tyng especially is familiar to all, and the thrilling watchword, "Stand up for Jesus," uttered by his son in a dying hour, furnished the inspiration of one of the sweetest songs of Zion, sung in every land and language where the story of the Cross is told.

### ERECTION OF "THE HALL."

Conference meetings and lectures were first held in private houses and in the Pastor's study or parlor; but at length the time arrived when a room in a private house no longer answered the wants of the people and resort was had successively to several halls.

The first hall used for this purpose was owned by Joseph Brown, Esq., and stood near the present site of the Methodist Church on State street. It was in the second story, and was also used as a school room by Mr. Wyatt Manchester until his decease. The lower story was used for storing lumber. This was known as the "Blue Hall," until it was sold, removed to "the Neck," and made over into a dwelling house.

On leaving the "Blue Hall," a small hall in the second story of another building on State street was rented for a short time, but it proving too strait for the wants of the people it was abandoned, and the Court house on the Common was obtained for use, excepting when needed for Court business.

This arrangement not proving satisfactory, measures were taken in the spring of 1821 to erect a Conference Hall. This was completed early in the winter of 1821-2, at a cost of about seven hundred and twenty dollars, under the supervision of Benjamin Wyatt, Benjamin Norris, and Giles Luther, as a Building Committee. It was located near the Parsonage, on the north side of Bradford street. It was a plain structure, measuring forty by thirty feet, with ten feet walls and an arched ceiling. It was furnished with plain wooden seats, but originally the seats on either side of the desk were considerably higher than the rest, and were occupied by the elder and more prominent members of the Church. One of the builders wished to have it called "Puritan Hall," and cut those words with considerable care on what he designed for the corner stone, but another with iconoclastic tendencies broke the stone in pieces with a maul, so the edifice was ever spoken of as simply "The Hall."

This Hall served the congregation for more than forty years, and was the scene of many seasons of spiritual refreshing. The farewell meeting held in it, 1870, February 20th, was one of peculiar interest. The room was filled to overflowing. The time was occupied with grateful reminiscences connected with the Hall, and with praise and prayer. After two hours thus occupied, all who had been converted in this Hall or by impressions received in it were requested to rise, and about one-third of the entire assembly responded. It was a most affecting testimony to the goodness of God experienced within those hallowed walls.

### ISAAC LEWIS, D. D.—EIGHTH PASTOR.

After the dismission of Mr. Mann, the hearts of the people turned to the REV. ISAAC LEWIS, D. D., whose labors in the Revival of 1812 were so signally blessed, by which he was greatly endeared to them. With hearty unanimity he was called to the Pastoral office and installed 1828, November 12th. He resided on Hope street, in the house now owned and occupied by the heirs of the late Major Jacob Babbitt. He remained in office until a failure of voice compelled him to retire, much to the regret of his people, 1831, September 28. After his dismission he resided in the family of his daughter in New York.

DR. LEWIS, and a brother ZECHARIAH, were twin sons of the Rev. Isaac Lewis, D. D., Sr., born in Wilton, Conn., 1773, January 1st, and were both graduated at Yale College in 1794.

The father was a son of a worthy and respectable farmer in Huntington, Conn., born in 1746, and graduated at Yale College in 1765. His conversion was during his junior year in college under the following remarkable circumstances: At that time the whole college was poisoned through the villainy of certain French neutrals. These fellows had taken mortal offence at the conduct of a few wild students, and, though every reasonable effort at reconciliation was made they refused to be reconciled, meditating the most deadly revenge. To accomplish their purpose they contrived to visit the kitchen at which the food of the students was prepared, and infused a large quantity of arsenic into one of the dishes that was to be placed before them. A deadly sickness came over all who had eaten of the dish, but by an immediate resort to medical aid most of them were cured, a few were so much affected that they died shortly after. Very soon after this the evangelist Whitefield visited New Haven, and preached in the College Chapel, and made use of this event as a solemn admonition. A profound impression was made upon the whole college, and many of the students were hopefully converted, among them the subject of this notice. After graduation he pursued theological studies under the direction of the Rev. Samuel Buell, of East Hampton, L. I., and of his pastor the Rev. Mr. Mills, of Huntington. Receiving calls to settle at Newport, R. I., and Wilton, Conn., he accepted the latter, and was ordained 1768, October 26th, and was married the same year to Hannah, eldest daughter of Matthew Beale, of New Preston, Conn., a lady every way suited to the station to which her marriage introduced her. During the Revolutionary struggle he espoused his country's cause with great zeal, served seven months as chaplain to one of the Connecticut regiments, and after the State troops were disbanded was appointed chaplain in the Continental army, but his people being unwilling to spare him again he declined thê appointment. A few years subsequent to this he labored arduously for a season in a missionary tour to the destitute fields in the vicinity of Dorset, Vt. During his residence in Wilton, he was invited to take charge of a congregation in South Carolina, but declined it, chiefly on the ground of his "strong disapprobation of the system of slavery." Becoming satisfied that the prevailing practice of "the half-way Covenant" was wrong, he took a stand against it, occasioning dissatisfaction among his people and finally leading to his dismission in June, 1786, after a Ministry of nearly eighteen years. On the day of his dismission he was invited to preach at Greenwich, Conn., and was soon after called to the Pastorate which he accepted, and was installed 1786, October 18th. After a highly successful ministry, by which he was greatly endeared to his people, he was dismissed, at his own urgent request, on account of the infirmities of age, 1818, December 1st, but he continued to dwell among his people, and to labor for their welfare as his strength would allow until his decease, 1840, August 27th, at the advanced age of nearly ninety-five years. In 1792 he received from his alma mater the degree of Doctor in Divinity. In 1816 he was chosen a member of the corporation of Yale College. He had a prominent agency in many of the benevolent movements of the day, and was connected with most of the prominent societies then existing for the extension of the Gospel and the promotion of the great interests of humanity. Dr. Lewis and his wife were the parents of nine children, six sons and three daughters. Of the five sons who lived to maturity, three were educated at Yale College, two entered the Ministry, and three were lawyers. Their mother died 1829, April 13th.

Zechariah, one of the twin brothers, studied theology at Philadelphia, Pa., and was, at the same time, a private tutor in the family of General Washington. In 1746 he was licensed to preach, but accepted the office of tutor in Yale College, where he continued until a failure of health compelled him to resign in the summer of 1799. Not recovering health sufficient to enter upon the Ministry, he became editor of "the Commercial Advertiser" and "New

York Spectator," and remained in this employment till about the year 1820. He was subsequently corresponding secretary of the "New York Religious Tract Society," and of the "United Foreign Mission Society;" and commenced and for several years edited the "American Missionary Register." He died at his residence in Brooklyn, N. Y., 1840, November 14th, in the sixty-eighth year of his age.

Dr. Lewis, our Pastor, pursued his theological studies at New Haven, under both Presidents Stiles and Dwight. He was ordained 1798, May 30th, and in 1800 was installed over the First Presbyterian Church in Cooperstown, N. Y., from whence he was called, in 1806, to the Presbyterian Church in Goshen, N. Y., and from there came to Bristol in 1812. After his brief but fruitful labors here, he officiated as stated supply in the Churches of New Rochelle and West Farms, N. Y., until he was called to succeed his venerable father at Greenwich, Conn., being installed on the day of his father's dismission, 1818, December 1st. After a remarkably successful Ministry of a few years he resigned his charge, and was soon after settled as the eighth Pastor in the line of succession over this ancient Church.

In 1844 he was honored with the degree of Doctor in Divinity by Delaware College. In 1827 he preached the Election Sermon at New Haven, Conn. Several sermons and public addresses were published, including the Ordination sermon of Rev. Joshua Knight, at Sherburne, Mass., 1804, two or three occasional sermons preached at Bristol, and an address before the Fairfield County Bible Society in 1844.

A man of excellent talents, of elevated Christian character, of fine expressive countenance, of urbane and gentlemanly manners, and of richly endowed and well furnished mind, he commanded the respect of all. As a preacher he was sound in doctrine, able and eloquent in appeal. As a Pastor he was faithful, and won the hearts of all who received his kind and Christian ministrations. He died at New York, 1854, September 23d, in the eighty second year of his age.

His Ministry in Bristol, though brief, was distinguished by another of those seasons of great spiritual refreshing which characterized this period, resulting in large accessions to the membership of the Church.

### THE REVIVAL OF 1830.

Though from advancing years the natural force of Dr. Lewis had in a degree abated, the recollection of his past services secured for him a warm welcome to the hearts of the people who were ready to co-operate with him in every good word and work. The thoroughly evangelical character of his preaching, his fidelity in pastoral labors, the sweet influence of his christian example, the kindly and prayerful co-operation of the Church prepared the way for a third general Revival in 1830, of a similar character and extent to the two which had preceded it. Respecting this great work of grace, we make no special record of incidents or details, but it is gratefully remembered by the surviving subjects of it as a precious season of interest throughout all the Churches, and affecting nearly every family in the town. The converts, numbered by hundreds, were of all ages and several of them were far advanced in life, who, having passed through the previous seasons of refreshing without submitting themselves to God, felt that this was a last call to them, and unless they now yielded to the Divine claims their day of grace was over.

Thus has God blessed this Church and town with repeated and remarkable Pentecostal seasons, and his blessing has rested upon the community at all times. Surely He is faithful that hath promised, and His mercies are from everlasting to everlasting. With what gratitude should we acknowledge his goodness, with what penitence should we acknowledge our sins before Him, with what earnest faith should we consecrate ourselves and all that we possess to His service.

## VIII.

## THE BUILDING STILL GOING FORWARD. 1830–1872.

### JOHN STARKWEATHER.—NINTH PASTOR.

The ninth Pastor in the succession was the Rev. John Starkweather, a native of Worthington, Mass.; a graduate of Yale College, 1825, and of Andover Theological Seminary. The call, voted on the 21st of November, 1831, was unanimons, and with cordial harmony he was duly installed on the 14th of December following. For a time this unanimity of feeling continued, but at length there arose considerable dissatisfaction and want of confidence which was expressed in a written communication to the Pastor, signed by twenty-one male members. On the 29th of December, 1834, the matter was mutually referred to an Ecclesiastical Council, who advised the dissolution of the Pastoral relation, which advice was accepted.

During his brief Ministry twenty-two were added to the Church, and the Manual which has been in use to the present time was prepared and published.

### THOMAS SHEPARD, D. D.—TENTH PASTOR.

Soon after the dismission of Mr. Starkweather, efforts were made to secure the services of the Rev. Thomas Shepard, late of Ashfield, Mass., and by a unanimous vote of the Church and Society he was called to the Pastoral office, 1835, April 1st. Accepting the call he was duly installed on the 30th of April following.

DR. SHEPARD was a native of Norton, Mass., born 1792, May 7th; graduated at Brown University 1813, and at Andover Theological Seminary 1816; was employed until 1819 as a missionary and teacher in the State of Georgia; and on the 16th of June, of that year, was ordained as Colleague Pastor with the venerable Nehemiah Porter over the Church, in Ashfield, Mass. After a successful ministry of about fourteen years, during which two hundred and seventy-four were admitted to his Church; he was dismissed 1833, May 8th. After his dismission from Ashfield, he was employed as an agent for the American Bible Society about two years, from which service he was called to the Pastorate here. In 1853 he received from Brown University the Degree of Doctor in Divinity. In 1846 he was elected a corporate member of the American Board of Commissioners for Foreign Missions.

A Parsonage was early in his Ministry erected on Bradford street, which he has occupied with his family ever since. A few years ago Mrs. Sarah W. Shepard, the sharer of his joys and burdens, was called to her home above. A devoted wife and mother, a faithful friend to all, and especially kind to the poor, a decided Christian in all the walks of life, her memory is cherished gratefully by the people among whom she passed her useful life.

On the 7th of May, 1865, he resigned the active duties and responsibilities of the Pastoral office, and asked that a successor might be chosen. His resignation was accepted, with the understanding that he would continue to live among his own people until called up higher, and the use of the Parsonage was tendered him during the remainder of his life. He still lives among us as the retired Pastor universally respected and beloved.

During his Ministry several seasons of unusual religious interest transpired. In 1837, 1838, 1842, 1846, 1852 and 1858, the Holy Spirit's power was manifested in the quickening of God's children and the conversion of many souls. These seasons are gratefully remembered by all who were participants in them.

### ERECTION OF THE THIRD HOUSE OF WORSHIP.

Early in 1855, the subject of erecting a new House of Worship was agitated, and, after some deliberation, it was decided to proceed to build. The following gentlemen were chosen a Building Committee, under whose supervision the work was successfully accomplished: William B. Spooner, Messadore T. Bennett, Josiah Gladding, Stephen T. Church, and Nathan Bardin.

The House is located on the corner of Bradford and High streets, fronting on the latter. It has three entrances in front and a rear entrance at the south-east corner leading to the library and pulpit, and also leading to the chapel recently built. It has a tower on the north-west corner eighteen feet square with buttresses extending upward about eighty feet, surmounted with belfrey and turrets. The full dimensions of the house are as follows: Length, one hundred and one feet; width, sixty-seven feet; walls, twenty-eight feet high in the clear, and thirty-nine feet from the floor to the apex of nave of the main arch. The style of architecture is gothic. The trimmings and buttresses are of pure granite; the filling up is of a stone somewhat different in quality, presenting a pleasing variety in figure and color. The roof is covered with slate and tin. The interior is finished with groin arched ceiling with eight pendants or corbels for springing the arches, and from which depend the chandeliers. The pews, numbering one hundred and fourteen on the main floor, are circular, trimmed with black walnut, and neatly upholstered. The pulpit, communion table and chairs are of black walnut, harmonising well with the general style of the house. The recess back of the pulpit is richly frescoed as are also the arches in the ceiling of the roof. The organ, made by Messrs. Hook, of Boston, is finished to correspond with the interior of the Church. The case is gothic, thirty-four feet high and fourteen feet wide. It has thirty-two registers or stops, and is of superior tone and capacity. The orchestra is dropped within a few feet of the main floor, and harmonizes in style with the pulpit at the opposite end. The entire floor of the Church is richly carpeted, and the whole interior is lighted with gas. The architect was Seth H.

Ingalls, and the master builder was William Ingalls, both of New Bedford, Mass.

The House stood complete and ready for dedication in November, 1856. On the 23d, farewell services of an interesting character including an historical discourse by the Pastor, founded on Psalm xlviii. 12-13, were held in the old House, and on the 25th the new House was dedicated to Almighty God with appropriate services including discourse by the Pastor, founded on Psalm lxxvii. 13. These were occasions of special interest to the congregation who requested copies of the discourses for publication, which request was complied with. The following extracts from these discourses will show the animating spirit of Pastor and people:

"In taking leave of these venerable walls within which our fathers have sat and listened to the messages of salvation for seventy-two years, where venerable men of God, some of whom have ceased from earth and gone to their final reward. have been trained for the kingdom of glory, where the praises of God have been sung by lips which are now responding to angelic harps around the throne, many affecting thoughts crowd themselves upon our minds. This has been the birth-place of souls. Here, blind eyes have been opened to behold the light of truth, as it shines in the face of Jesus. Here deaf ears have been unstopped to listen with rapture to the messages of mercy through atoning blood. Here multitudes have set out in the christian race, for the prize of an unfading crown. Oh! how hallowed to memory is such a place. But it has done its work, and in the revolutions of time it is meet that it should give place to another, and a more commodious and more attractive house of worship. And while the very dust of this sanctuary will ever remain precious in our eyes, may our united prayers ascend to God, that the glory of the latter house may exceed the glory of the former. The materials of its walls are imperishable. Long, long will it resist the corroding tooth of time. Centuries will not impair those granite foundations, scores of generations will worship in its courts, and thousands of the sanctified pass up to the purer devotions of heaven."

"What is this new and stately edifice, this pulpit, these pews, yonder orchestra, these frescoed arches? What but one common passage way to the grave, the judgment seat, the retributions of eternity. If they all could speak to us, would not their united voice be "Prepare to meet thy God?" Oh if these buttresses and turrets and pillars and arches and gildings had a tongue to speak for Him, to whose service they are this day dedicated, they would say to you in tones unearthly, 'let not the novelty of these imposing scenes divert your minds one moment from the great question, What must I do to be saved?' Consecrated stone or wood or mortar wrought into the highest state of architectural symmetry and beauty cannot save you. Yonder organ with its deep and silvery tones, this pulpit with the highest eloquence that shall ever grace it, cannot, of themselves, work out your salvation. Except ye repent and believe in the Lord Jesus Christ,—except ye give your heart to God and live to His glory, ye must live and die without hope. No external privileges can supercede the necessity of the washing of regeneration and the renewing of the Holy Ghost."

"See that you refuse not Him that speaketh to you today through these scenes and services. Bring no strange fire to offer on this altar. Come up hither with the sacrifice of an humble and contrite heart. Listen to the Word as those who must give account. Pray with a fervent spirit. Make melody in your hearts unto the Lord. In a word, worship God in spirit and in truth. And after a few more Sabbath suns shall have arisen and set, you will have offered your last prayer, have sung your last hymn of praise, joined in your last communion service, your seat be occupied by another, and your spirit, if purified in the blood of the Lamb, will pass away to the Sanctuary above,

> Where the assembly ne'er breaks up
> And the Sabbath ne'er shall end."

### CYRUS P. OSBORNE.—ELEVENTH PASTOR.

After the retirement of Dr. Shepard, several persons were heard as candidates for settlement until the 11th of September, 1865, when the Church voted unanimously to call the Rev. Cyrus P. Osborne, in which action the Society also concurred, and on the 2d of November following, he was duly ordained and installed as the Eleventh Pastor in the succession.

Mr. Osborne was born in East Boston, Mass., graduated at Harvard College, 1859, and at Andover Theological Seminary, 1862. He continued in the Pastoral office until 1870, June 6th, when, at his own request, he was dismissed, that he might avail himself of a favorable opportunity to visit Europe and the Holy Land.

His ministry, though brief, was fruitful in good results. An interesting revival of religion was enjoyed in 1866-67, during which season a large number of young persons professed conversion, and over a hundred united with the Church on profession of faith.

## PAYMENT OF THE DEBT.

One leading object in the organization of the Catholic Society was to secure a permanent fund for the support of the Ministry. With much self-denial a fund was started which promised to be of very material aid by a prospective increase from year to year. But the event did not justify the hopes thus entertained. Eighteen years later the fund seems to have shrank somewhat, for in the settlement with Dr. Wight a note of one thousand dollars was given by the Society. This beginning of debt was a bad precedent too easily followed in subsequent years, until it rolled up in round numbers to six thousand dollars. On the 22d of March, 1864, a member of the Society, who has since rested from his earthly labors, liberally offered "to pay one-half the debt himself if the Society would raise by subscription a like sum." This offer set the people to thinking, but did not arouse them sufficiently to secure the desired end until the fall of 1867, when, at a meeting in "the Hall," on the evening of September 17, about forty members of the congregation being present, the ball was set in motion by a liberal subscription, a committee was appointed to canvass the parish, and in a few weeks the requisite amount was secured. Great was the rejoicing over this result, and a meeting of the people for thanksgiving and praise was appointed, which was attended by large numbers and is spoken of as "the Jubilee meeting."

### ERECTION OF THE MEMORIAL CHAPEL.

The year following the payment of the Society's debt, the subject of erecting a Chapel was agitated, "the Hall" being thought by many to be too small for the present and prospective need of the Church. The Sabbath School began to make weekly offerings as the nucleus of a fund for this purpose, and plans were discussed of securing a general contribution throughout the congregation, but before arrangements were completed, two sisters who had often made the Church their debtor by their unstinted benefactions, desiring to honor their sainted parents and at the same time make provision for the wants of the Church, whose spiritual welfare was dear to them, assumed the entire responsibility of building and furnishing a "Memorial Chapel." Arrangements were soon completed, and the work was begun under the supervision of Messadore T. Bennett, William B. Spooner, William H. Church, Stephen T. Church, Martin Bennett, and James E. French, as a building committee. The architect was Seth Ingalls, Esq., of New Bedford, Mass. The corner stone was laid with appropriate services at eleven o'clock, Tuesday, July 6th, 1869, and in the following February the Chapel stood complete and furnished for occupancy.

The Chapel adjoins the Church edifice, with which it harmonizes in material and style. The walls are of rubble stone; the door, windows and buttresses of dressed granite. The side walls are thirteen feet, and the main gable thirty-four feet high. The ceiling is finished to the height of twenty-nine feet. A vestibule ten feet by eleven feet joins the Chapel to the Church. A north wing extends across the end of the vestibule and in the rear of the Church twenty-six feet by twenty-two feet two inches. A south wing projects from the opposite side fifteen feet by twenty-one feet eight inches. The main audience room, with which the wings are connected by sliding doors with ground glass panels, is thirty-three feet by fifty feet. These are all inside measurements. The floors are of southern pine laid in mortar. The walls are ceiled up thirty inches from the floor with southern pine. having a base and chair moulding of black walnut. The ceiling overhead is finished with transverse arches and pendants or corbels for springing the arches to which are attached the gas fixtures. The walls above the chair moulding and the ceiling overhead are neatly tinted with a light color that harmonizes well with the general style of the interior. The western or front gable has a large gothic window of stained glass, and a similar window of ground glass is in the north gable. The other windows are all of ground glass.

The main audience room is furnished with black walnut seats in cast iron frames with reversible backs, a neat black walnut desk made by William O. and Charles Manchester, and gothic chairs of the same material for the platform, a small black walnut table front of the desk, and a Mason & Hamlin organ, valued at three hundred dollars, presented by the Sabbath School. The aisles and the space front of the seats and around the platform are covered with neat and durable matting, and the platform with a tasteful carpet. The north room is furnished with settees with reversible backs, and a movable desk and chairs, and the entire floor is neatly carpeted. The south room is carpeted similar to the north room, and is furnished with an extension table and movable chairs. By opening the sliding doors the three rooms are thrown into one, every part of which is in range with the desk of the large room.

Upon the inner wall of the large room is a plain marble tablet, inscribed as follows:

THIS CHAPEL

DEDICATED TO THE SERVICE OF GOD, THE FATHER, SON, AND HOLY GHOST,

WAS ERECTED IN 1869, IN MEMORY OF

WILLIAM AND CHARLOTTE DEWOLF,

DECEASED 1829.

BY THEIR DAUGHTERS CHARLOTTE DEWOLF AND MARIA DEWOLF ROGERS.

*" We have thought of thy loving kindness*
*O God in the midst of thy temple."*

The Chapel was dedicated 1870, February 24th, with impressive services, including a dedicatory address by the pastor, Mr. Osborne, and dedicatory prayer by Dr. Shepard.

The address closed as follows:

"Thus, my hearers, does this occasion suggest to us important duties, too apt to be neglected. Does it not also call for grateful acknowledgments; first to God, whose providence has furnished us this gift; next to the human instruments of His benefaction.

"It is pleasant to commend. To praise the patience and wise council of the building committee, the skill of the architect and builder, the fidelity of the workmen in their several parts, the zeal of one who has shown the deepest interest in the difficult work of furnishing the several apartments were a grateful office and not embarrassing. But worthily to praise the bountiful devotion which has built these walls and given this edifice, with all its comely furnishings, a free-will offering to the Lord,—for this I have no fitting words. I cannot give voice to the grateful sentiments that pervade this assembly. Nor would I if I could. For this would only wound the tender sensibilities of natures as modest as they are munificent.

"We will only rejoice that their eyes have been permitted to behold their completed offering, and to be witnesses of our joy in its completion; and pray they may be spared to see it become according to their fervent wish, 'the birthplace of souls,' and resolve never to forget their frequently expressed desire, that this sanctuary may be hallowed to the service of the Master.

"There is an element in this offering too sacred for our touch. 'In Memoriam' is graved upon its walls, pointing our thoughts heavenward.

> 'Oh, it is sweet to think of those that are departed,
> While numbered prayers sink to silence tender-hearted;
> While tears that leave no pain, are tranquilly distilling,
> And the dead live again, in hearts that love is filling.'

"Some will make the dead live again in flowers upon their grave, watered with tears that have their fountains in the heart. Some will keep their name alive by tons of rock heaped over them,—marble from Italy or granite from the hills, carved into elegant but idle forms. But far more beautiful is that affection which turns the memory of the dead into a benediction of the living. It was a loving thought of the sainted dead that reared this little temple. It was a happy thought that combined in a single act such honor to the memory of parents long departed, and such devotion to a Redeemer's cause. If the redeemed in heaven can witness earthly scenes, those revered parents must rejoice, as piety and filial love now lay this offering at Immanuel's feet."

### JAMES P. LANE.—TWELFTH PASTOR.

On the first Sabbath in November, 1870, the present Pastor began to preach as a candidate for settlement. Receiving a unanimous call from the Church and Society, he accepted the same, and on the 11th of January, 1871, was duly installed in office. The sermon on this occasion was by the Rev. Jacob M. Manning, D. D., of Boston, Mass. The installing prayer was by the Rev. John L. Taylor, D. D., of Andover, Mass.

Mr. Lane was a native of Candia, N. H.; son of the late Isaiah Lane, M. D., who deceased at Meriden, N. H., in 1855. He graduated at Amherst College, 1857, pursued Theological studies at Andover, and was ordained pastor of the Congregational Church in East Weymouth, Mass., 1861, January 10th. After a ministry of nearly five years, during which about one hundred were admitted to the Church, he was called to the pastorate of the Free Church in Andover, and was installed 1866, April 4th. From Andover he removed to Bristol.

## CHARITABLE FUNDS AND CONTRIBUTIONS.

A bequest of five hundred dollars, made by MRS. ANN COGGESHALL, widow of William Coggeshall, and deposited in "the Bristol Institution for Savings," is held in trust by the treasurer for the benefit "of needy widows who are communicants and members of the Church," and the annual interest is distributed to those who are entitled to receive it on or about the first of January in each year. This fund became first available in 1855.

In 1867, November 6th, MRS. MARY T. B. GLADDING, (the founder of the Sabbath School in 1816,) deceased, aged eighty-two years. After other bequests, she gave to the Church the rest of her property, amounting to about five hundred dollars, to be forever held in trust for "the use and benefit of aged and indigent females, communicants of the Church." This fund is deposited in "the Bristol Institution for Savings," and the annual interest is distributed according to the terms of the bequest by the pastor at his discretion.

The late B. W. GREENE, ESQ., of Hartford, Conn., made a bequest of property, valued at about two thousand dollars, "to the poor of the Church congregation in Bristol, R. I., the proceeds or income to be distributed annually by the Deacons of the Church." The Will containing this bequest was set aside by the Probate Court, but the heirs generously undertook to carry out the intentions of the testator in an agreement to pay over the amount "to the Congregational Church in Bristol, R. I., in trust that the income shall be annually spent for the poor of said Church at their discretion." This fund, amounting to about two thousand two hundred dollars, is deposited in "the Mechanic's Savings Bank, Providence," and in "the Providence Institution for Savings," the bank books being in the hands of the Church Treasurer.

Collections for the poor are taken at each communion season, and distributed by the Deacons at their discretion; also, an annual collection for the same object at the time of the State and National Thanksgiving.

With these liberal provisions for the poor—supplemented by other private benefactions,—the Church is also mindful of the calls for religious and charitable work abroad. The causes of Home and Foreign Missions, Christian Education, Bible dissemination, etc., receive annual attention, and contributions amounting in the aggregate to several hundreds of dollars are made. A "Ladies Missionary Society," connected with the Church, contribute, besides donations in money, articles of clothing, etc., auxiliary to both the Home Missionary and Foreign Missionary Boards of our denomination.

A "Sewing School" has been sustained by several of the ladies of our congregation, and much good accomplished in teaching poor children this useful art, and providing needed garments which are given them.

There are other local charities in the support of

which this Church unites, with the other religious societies in town, as follows:

A "Home for destitute Children," under the care of a matron and the supervision of a board of lady managers, selected from the various religious societies in town. The current expenses of this noble charity are met chiefly by the voluntary contributions of the citizens annually. The house and garden for the Home were the gift of the late Robert Rogers, Esq., of our congregation. A thousand dollars, also, from the same estate, has been placed at interest for the benefit of this institution.

A "Ladies Charitable Society," embracing members from all the Churches, has existed for many years, and through this agency great good is accomplished in ministering to the wants of the worthy poor.

A "Young Men's Christian Association" maintain a public reading room and library, accessible to all under certain regulations. The current expenses are met by the dues of members and voluntary contributions.

A "Bible Committee," auxiliary to the American Bible Society, keep a depository of Bibles and Testaments which are sold at cost, or given to the destitute who are unable to buy.

### SACRAMENTAL FURNITURE.

A massive Baptismal Font of white sand stone, beautifully wrought, was presented to the Church by

Rev. Prof. J. Lewis Diman, of Providence, and stands near the pulpit in the House of Worship.

The Communion service is of solid silver, and includes two cups inscribed "as the gift of Nathaniel Byfield, 1693;" one cup "the gift of Rev. John Sparhawk, 1718;" three cups "to the Bristol Non-Conformist Church, March 29, 1723," the donor of which is not known; two cups "the gift of Hon. Nathaniel Blagrove, 1745;" and two flagons, presented August, 1855, by Miss Charlotte DeWolf, and Mrs. Maria DeWolf Rogers.

This book is a preservation photocopy.
It was produced on Hammermill Laser Print natural white,
a 60 # book weight acid-free archival paper
which meets the requirements of
ANSI/NISO Z39.48-1992 (permanence of paper)

Preservation photocopying and binding
by
Acme Bookbinding
Charlestown, Massachusetts
1995

CPSIA information can be obtained
at www.ICGtesting.com
Printed in the USA
LVHW040059230323
742312LV00002B/34

9 783382 128111